Places in the World
a Woman Could Walk

Places in the World
a Woman Could Walk

stories by Janet Kauffman

ALFRED A. KNOPF

NEW YORK 1983

THIS IS A BORZOI BOOK
PUBLISHED BY ALFRED A. KNOPF, INC.

With thanks to the Michigan Council for the Arts and the Corporation
of Yaddo, for their support, and to the editors of *Antaeus*, *Soho News*,
Tri-Quarterly, and *Vanity Fair*, where some of these stories appeared in
slightly different form; and to the editors of *The New Yorker*, where "Patriotic" originally appeared.   J.K.

Library of Congress Cataloging in Publication Data
Kauffman, Janet. Places in the world a woman could walk.
Contents: Places in the world a woman could walk—
My mother has me surrounded—Isn't it something?— [etc.]
I. Title.
PS3561.A82P5 1983   813'.54   83-47672
ISBN 0-394-52996-0

Manufactured in the United States of America
First Edition

For Jamie

Contents

Places in the World
a Woman Could Walk

Places in the World
a Woman Could Walk

The day the tornado hit Morenci was the day Lady Fretts finally put her mind to the slaughter of Susie Hey Susie and her Babies. I said good. I said do. Enough of holdover, mournful faces. The Babies had lived out a dozen years, on borrowed time, interest-free. They were Lady's chief souvenirs. Each day it was my job to feed them—Susie Hey Susie, the cow we had never milked; and her Babies, thriving for nobody's benefit and beefed up to one thousand pounds apiece.

Lady said, "Molly, I think I can stand it."

Our knees nearly touched. In green storm light and early dark, I wanted like never before to believe the sweet set of her mouth. Lady loomed and spread, magnanimous, wrapped in her green quilted robe, set in an old kitchen chair in the corner of the basement. She tipped the chair back against the whitewashed

stone foundation. Oh, she was my Buddha, my jade dispro-
portionate buddy. Her legs, I can say it, were too short. But Lady
was tall through the torso, with a wide back and a strength of
body that looked spiritual. Cross-legged or lounging, she reigned
like a plunked-down legitimate deity who knew that walking could
give the appearance of too great an involvement with the earth.

"They want better now!" she shouted at me. "They've taken
a grief and groaned with it. It's been my pleasure to fatten them,
Molly. My real pleasure!"

"I know it." More thunder hit.

"What?"

"Yes!" I said.

Lady cupped her hands to her mouth and hollered over the
winds, "I think I can stand it!" Then she put her palms to her
ears to block off the racket.

So do it before the orchard flowers, I thought, but was not
about to say, because Lady was a woman to be acknowledged
and nothing more. It was her habit, anyway, in later more generous spring, to decide instead: some things must simply live and
feast. There'd be a reprieve. I'd dip out more feed. Nonetheless,
I understood that one day she'd go right on through with the
sentence. Lady wasn't a fool; she knew Susie Hey Susie and her
Babies were not immortals. She knew there were limits.

But I'm an agreeable person, an old-time henchman sort of
person, which Lady demanded. When Lady made up her mind,
I got things done. She bragged about me, the sister of her dead
husband, her gone-but-sustained Wil-Johnny, and the bragging
puffed us both up. I wasn't obliged to join in. Or obligated to
add any words for her. The whole of Morenci envisioned Lady
Fretts as an obvious darling and good fat widow. She's all that
she looks, they formulated. Look again, I'd have to say.

. . .

We sat out the storm and its whamming against the cellar's west window, the two of us solid, fixed in consideration of the fate of Susie Hey Susie and her twin bloated Babies, the three of them probably standing nose to nose in the barn.

I'd ushered Lady into the cellar at eight, and she liked the care that I took, the extra batteries and pillows, the tote bag of mint-wafer Girl Scout cookies, and soda water, and clear plastic glasses. The whole outside pitched and reeled. The barn would be singing.

Lady sat with the flashlight propped in her lap, its light riding between her breasts and spanning out on her face. After a while she shut her eyes like someone ordained to sleep through catastrophe as a point of dogma, and I took up her plan where she'd left it, at the beginning. I had in mind the order of calls: Lam for the truck and loading; Alfred Torello for the slaughter itself— he'd know the tankage place in Adrian to take it from there.

Lady crossed her arms on her stomach in sleep. She could be reconsidering; I took that into account. But she lifted her lids in the first precarious light, and moved her lips: "We should bury them here."

"You don't want to see them dead."

"I saw Wil-Johnny dead, and his eye was a cinder. I'm able."

"We'd need a backhoe."

"I want them here in the orchard. You understand, Molly, it's my wish. That would be the best way." She stood up and yoked the blanket over her shoulders. She left it to me.

These were simpler arrangements, in spite of her sentiment: call Dahlia Smith for the backhoe work, and Alfred Torello for the kill. Lady Fretts drew herself on with sentiment. She had no reason for anything—but sure-fire emotion. She'd lived her life like the unblemished blind, by feeling. She *loved* Wil-Johnny, yes; she loved Susie Hey Susie, his Jersey cow; and these were the curlicue loves that wound on and on and twisted to stuff of the world with multiple tendrils. Not much escaped. Love grew and it grew, according to Lady's law. Love manifested itself in expansive forms, and in weight, and in hefty creatures of the world.

Susie Hey Susie was stuffed as a heart.

Twelve years ago, Wil-Johnny walked by the left horn, Lady by the right, through the flowering tangled orchard the day before he died, struck down where he stood by broken-off, flung lightning, that Lady said split from the Golden Delicious trunk and fell more like a limb than fire on his amazed face. Lady was glad she had seen it; it had given her courage, she said.

The day after Wil-Johnny died, I moved in, and it wasn't exactly a favor. Mother, who'd apparently waited for years for Wil-Johnny's independence, packed the tote bag and pushed me on. "Lady will need you, Molly, for some good while. Do what you can. I only play mama for sons."

I saw what she meant when a couple of weeks after that she flew for the first time, Detroit nonstop to Bermuda. She'd never talked travel with me.

It was as if the whole world unshackled itself. Wil-Johnny's smiting flashed light across everyone's naked face. My own mother shook herself free. Lady Fretts caught me up and, from then to now, advised me in handling her heartfelt missions. She explained her love for Wil-Johnny and she taught me a quick way to recognize love. She taught me to drive a car, to bid at auctions, to plow.

And I muscled. I saw clear enough where I stood—in the middle—and what I was, too—the right hand of Lady. I said to myself, at the start: Molly is no gaggle blond. Molly is working.

Molly, as usual, was biding her time.

I was part of the newest order, inaugurated the night of Wil-

Johnny's funeral, with a momentous birth: Susie Hey Susie delivered her twin heifers, a double amazement. Lady, in large and sentimental measure, announced that Susie Hey Susie and her Babies—and Molly, too, she said—were *gifts*, new lives in a dour time. Auspicious lives. Lady told me she was determined to grieve, and to grow, too. I said then—I've said all along—that makes sense. It felt like a baptism, her sprinkling of words.

Lady managed well, without romance, a small-time *grande dame*, domiciled of her own free will in a three-room shingled house. Days, she kept to her Wil-Johnny bed, with magazines and cards, or she moved herself out to the living room and cushioned herself on the brown sofa. At night, I slept posted by her door like a down-and-out bodyguard on that sofa. Cats had got at it and torn the arms with their claws.

Except for the stove, which I kept open in a side-room kitchen, the house was Lady's closet, her store of pastel sweaters and magazines and stacks of board games. The walls of the basement were clean and solid, but the rest of the place to my mind was ramshackle and clotted. If I complained, Lady said, "Don't worry. The mind is clear." Her color T.V. washed the world such an unnatural orange we couldn't watch. "We have events of our own," Lady said.

In good light, I followed Lady upstairs. The tornado had cut through Morenci—out the living-room window, we could see, on the horizon, three halves of houses and a simple path notched with the white glimmering scars of torn trees. Out the other way, in the orchard, two trees were down, which left four others standing, and those had the beaten look of trees at high altitudes. The lawn was a wreck of shingles, green asphalt ones from the house, wood shingles from the barn, and tar-paper shreds from someplace I never figured. There were wide purple streamers snagged in the mulberry tree, like strips from a crashed kite, or the shameful debris of flood, hanging and drying.

On my way out to feed the animals, I found a blue dress on the barbed-wire fence by the orchard. But the barn, which deserved to be slapped by the wind like a hand, and which would have collapsed at the touch, stood there unmarred. When I stepped onto the driveway, Susie Hey Susie and her Babies thrust their enormous heads through the east side of the barn, at their usual gaping holes. The three were indifferent swooners, outsized, and no good. Susie Hey Susie was a little broader of face, with a wide swatch over the left eye. She kept that eye on me, a patient eye. I fed them and offered some warning: This is it. Time's up.

I cleaned up the yard and burned trash before I called Dahlia to dig the graves. She'd come, she said, right away. In a couple of hours the shock would roll away in Morenci and some real work would open up. She'd finish this small job first.

In the living room, Lady lounged on the sofa with her teacup in both hands, steadying herself, I think, for a walk out the back door. I gave her a tally of losses and damage, and mentioned the blue dress as part of the chronicle.

"Is it worth keeping?"

"I burned it." That was the kind of thing I did on my own.

"A blue dress can tell you more than a few things, Molly. You should have brought it in." Pronouncing from the rolls of her quilted green robe.

"It was cotton, a girl's size," I said. But there I was, pouring more hot water for her, anticipating an account of blue dresses and the whole truth. She tugged and bit off a thread from her robe, as if she'd been taught the skill in handmaiden school.

About ten-thirty, Dahlia rolled in the drive and went right on through to the orchard, where I met her and pointed out the three grave sites Lady had specified, each one a point in a triangle around a long-fallen cherry tree, Susie Hey Susie's favorite. The trunk was sheared of bark, and rubbed smooth from the cow's daily sidelong massages. She leaned there for hours.

Susie Hey Susie's prolonged and monotonous life was Lady's concoction of bliss: sweet timothy hay in the morning, aquamarine and tufted; the orchard all day, in every weather but blizzard, the rub there of hide and wood; slow stomping; sleep in simple shade; a magical lifting of tail and the steamy torrents of soft waste pooling in deep circles; enormous Babies close as the trees, drifting but never wandering; and the purposeless growth of them all toward some blithe exchange with earth and sky.

I couldn't see real evidence of love, or of grief, for that matter, in them. But it was an aromatic, goodly world. "I appreciate their coincidence," Lady told me. And therein was the grace that cradled them all.

I lulled along, too.

Dahlia dug the three pits in less than an hour, trenching, dumping, building neat conical heaps of fill by the sides of the graves. I don't suppose the hook she had for a right hand really helped her any, but to my eye it seemed to, at least when she worked the backhoe. She attached herself to the machine with special clamps she'd screwed onto the wheel and onto the levers. Click. No bend in the wrist. More clicks, here we go.

I invited her in for tea.

"Are you giving up Wil-Johnny, then?" Dahlia asked Lady. "You don't mind?" Dahlia clamped her hook on the tea-bag string and lifted it out.

"I've got him secure. I can give up reminders. That is the way I see it now," Lady said in her turnabout voice.

"Well, it won't be the same place. The Babies!" Dahlia sighed, very heavy.

"*You* mourn, if you must," Lady smiled. She leaned back.

With a twist of the whole hooked hand, Dahlia flipped her empty cup upside down in the saucer, a kind of a show, in parting. Dahlia was one of those arrogant, thick-thighed women the mucklands around Morenci kick up. She tapped her heels when she left, like a war hero, nicely decorated.

Lady Fretts had worldly, show-off qualities, too—although she didn't appear to do a thing. It was a talent, complementary, I think, to the unenterprising ways of men like Wil-Johnny. "Yeah, I got that straight," he'd say, flatly. "Yeah, you got that right."

Lady says that I spit when I walk, like Wil-Johnny.

I have this, too, in common with my brother: I tire out right at the end of the day and sleep very well.

Wil-Johnny claimed that he never dreamed, except of himself asleep in variously pillowed scenes. It was restful, he said, both sleeps, this one and the one in the dream. Wil-Johnny took Lady's hand, though, and that was the first dose of lightning he suffered.

Alfred Torello came at one.

"I have no inclination," Lady said, "to attend," and she sat the episode out, acting deaf, on the sofa with the *Citizen Patriot* and a box of Fandangle cookies.

Alfred Torello and I pulled Susie Hey Susie and her Babies from the barn, into the orchard, and tethered them to limbs as near to the pits as we could. The day was very mild, with an unwavering blue sky, the blessèd blue a sky can color itself after the shock of storms.

Alfred Torello had a skill at slaughter so practiced it looked like chance. With the first of the Babies, he spread his palm across the forehead, a casual gesture, then drew back his rifle and fired one clean shot, point-blank. The heifer slumped, and his hand helped guide the fall to the right, by the digging. He stepped around her to the next hole—he paused, straightened, and arranged himself—then he repeated the gesture, the shot, the hand guiding, as the second Baby fell. And then, the third touch, the third shot, and the collapse of Susie Hey Susie, last.

Well. Decisions have their effects. Alfred Torello headed off toward his truck.

"Tell Lady it's done," I said, "and call Dahlia back."

I wasn't doing a thing.

I sat down on the tree trunk, in the midst. Susie Hey Susie and her Babies, large lumps, made a fuller impression dead than alive. They were mountainous; and unfooted, they assumed the repose of boulders in the grass. They managed an appropriate camouflage, natural as light and shade and rocks in any spring orchard.

I could report to Lady of the ease of their decline. A good many things were broken that morning, but Susie Hey Susie and her Babies, in their immensity, showed nothing of fracture or loss. To Lady, I knew it well, their deposit in memory, her hoard of mementos, would make them more dear: she favored each thing as some monument to some other, some souvenir.

It was hard not to see events through Lady's eyes. I looked around, for myself. Off toward Morenci, a miniature fire truck extended its ladder to the second floor of a broken house. There was no smoke, no flame, only the brown of the house, askew, the small red of the truck, and a dot of a man on the ladder.

Dahlia Smith waved herself in, the backhoe roaring, and she did a fair, quick job of pushing the bodies over the edge and filling the pits. I raked the domed surfaces smooth, and then I went in to get Lady for whatever it was she intended next.

Alfred Torello was pouring hot water in cups. Lady sat in her robe, wide and upright on the sofa. Her face summarized a calm; she looked up with an indeterminate slow gaze, and her cheeks rounded back into short curls of wood-colored brown hair. She stood up and moved as she sometimes could, without any suggestion of legs.

"Follow along, Molly. Alfred Torello will say a few words."

They passed me in the doorway. Alfred Torello took Lady's arm at the back step; he hiked up his shoulders with real effort and stepped very neatly over the driveway. He lent an intelligent, sensitive look to his face—it took shape with some crinkling around the eyes and the dropping down of his jaw so the lips grew fuller.

I followed them into the orchard, and we stopped at Susie Hey Susie's grave. Lady crossed her arms and stuffed her hands up the sleeves of the green robe.

Alfred Torello stepped forward a few feet, away from Lady, and he lifted his arm. He spread out his palm toward the blue, aiming. Then he raised his rifle and fired. The shot cracked through the blue sky, and I stepped back from that grave.

"Goddamn!" he said, loud, happy as amen.

Lady shook his hand, and they turned to walk back. Although it wasn't what I'd expected, I think the ceremony turned out exactly as Lady planned.

"Molly," Lady said to me later, some weeks later, when smells in the air said June. "I want a memorial."

"Let the grass do."

"I want this, Molly. Now, take my word. I'll carve up that trunk. It's there in the middle, just where it should be. Everything's right there, and I've done some carving. Anyway, I can think on it now. This weather, I should be out of doors."

Out of doors.

In a couple of days, she got to it. The whole planet tipped her way, and those were unsteady days for me. She was at unnatural labor, and not a woman I found comfortable to watch. Her idea was to carve out a likeness from the fallen trunk, a thing with horns and withers and rump, a slimmed-down Susie Hey Susie, hoofs tucked under. Once, Lady had whittled and sanded two wooden spoons, a crafty background she said served her well. And so I got her an ax and some chisels, and there she was.

"Work is a wonder, Molly," she said one day during a break. "I'm enjoying the weather. I've noticed a difference in breathing." She inhaled, and ballooned herself.

I was not impressed with her pleasure, which thrummed a monotonous familiar tone. She could stitch grand meaning, like golden thread, into the plainest hackwork. She'd pulled herself out of the house, and the rooms were slurs without her, three unraveling bags for cats. The house had a cavey flavor and dankness, somebody else's root cellar.

I ended up drinking my tea on the back step; Lady herself gave up tea altogether. A small pile of squeezed tea bags, with limp strings and paper flaps trailing, heaped up in the yard by my step. Something would cart them away to a hole, one of these days.

Lady moved from one skin into another; she had the same look, but brighter, glossier. From the back step, I watched her those mornings, and she looked like a born-again cowgirl out there on the trunk, riding it like you'd ride some mount, her green quilted robe pulled up to her knees and her legs like muscled arms, hugging a rough soul. She slung the ax with precision, shaping ears. Then she switched to the large chisel and red-handled hammer, and sloughed off long whitened wood curls with the gentleness of a barber. She leaned forward and sanded the surface, and rubbed it the way she had once rubbed the hide of Susie Hey Susie and her Babies.

It was hard for me to stand up and pick up a hoe. Hard for me to dig at the ground.

By July, Lady had put on shorts and a polka-dot halter top.

There were many particulars—of dress, of food, of ultimate purpose—that Lady and I evaded in evening discussions. She wanted to talk about art. She had me check out books from the library on statuary, on woodworking. At night, she leafed through the books, and the shiny pages of photographs reflected the light from the lamp onto her chin. It was clear Lady was dissatisfied with her work. She showed me a picture of a marble bull, his eyes empty sockets. "Admire that hoof, Molly. Look." She pointed. "I intend to do them justice," she said.

I could see fixed in her brain Susie Hey Susie and her Babies, their sides still warm and their faces moist.

"You gave them a dozen years, that's justice enough," I said.

She should have seen them on their sides on the ground, and remembered that.

"I know what I'm doing," Lady said. "I've read the books."

One day she was packing.

"Molly, I'm going to see how sculpting is done."

"Sculpting? Going how?"

"I'm flying, Molly. You remember your mama's card from Greece?"

"The naked Wil-Johnny man?"

"That's the one. I'm going to Athens, Greece."

Greece.

It was certainly as easy as Lady imagined: one call to Alfred Torello and she had a ride to Bisbee Travel, and the next day a ride to Metro.

That's all I know now.

I should hear something soon.

A woman makes up her mind these days, and life turns right around, pulls out like cartoon knitting.

For the time being, I'm cleaning the premises, airing rooms. Maybe she'll want the house boarded up.

I'll get a call.

Or she'll send me something—a rock, an armless woman like one in the books.

Lady rode a sofa for years; I should have seen it would be no trouble for her to take it from there. I might have known there were places in the world that woman could walk, sure-footed, and look powerful.

My Mother Has
Me Surrounded

At Rehoboth Beach, my mother digs her heels in the sand, faces the ocean, and, on her own cue, collapses on her back beside me.

"Are you all right?" I ask.

"Yes, sweetheart. Don't worry."

Water collects in the shadows beneath her knees. Every time she breathes, another rush of water pools there. I'm small enough to lie beside her and use her shade. There, I am invisible; I am in hiding, in the only darkness she offers me. But if I raise my head and look over my chin into the daylight, I can see the blond unshaven hair on her calves, glitters of sand among the hairs, and beyond her legs, clear strips of navy-blue ocean and white sky. The things I see have, as frame, one of my mother's limbs; that's how she places herself, convenient, dismembered, for such compositions. She doesn't realize that her body is breakable, but for me each glimpse of her, whole, is a resurrection. I believe it is she, not I, who attaches her body this closely at the edge of everything. When I look up, there is an arm, a leg: she points, or kicks, or lays claim, in my view, to all that she can.

It is early August. We lie in slopes in the dune—lounge-chair slopes we have carved out by hand. Nearer the water, a few sunbathers stretch out their arms and legs on striped towels; and along the wet shore close to the waves, two babies crouch like penguins and work at towers in the sand. Nobody bothers my mother.

I happen to be beside her—I happen to be her child, and she acknowledges this, sometimes rubbing my back with the oiled palms of her hands. She cups my shoulders and slides her palms down my arms. All the same, I'm a ghost to her. Lightweight. I hover, physically apparent since birth, but not yet fully attached to the world, not weighted with the bodily form she values: working thighs, an emphatic pelvis.

I am not aware of my bones—and I know this now, as I may have known it then, when she hugged me routinely and I hugged back, holding her ribs or sometimes the bones of her arms. The memory of embrace is the memory of breakneck collision. I am feeble, and my mother is knuckled and ankled like other Mennonite women, constructed to break ground, to dig. She bends over and around me, with the interior light, gray and green, of her approach, and the salt air from under her arms—a tent settling over center poles when forest light, daylight, separate from us, is shut out. She brings the artificial light of her own bones and skin. I live like a camper, off of the roads, homeless by somebody's choice. My face is scrubbed. I am unemployed, and nobody's lackey. Except hers. Whatever she knows about digging—digging to China, gravedigging—I am too thin and too timid to comprehend. It is my own mistake that I recognize my arms and belly as skin, as flesh, while she shakes my shoulders with her hands and says, oh, my baby. Her thumbs can press against any bone they choose.

But my mother's shoulders are fleshed and rounded, the firm shoulders of a swimmer; and for this, she is a scandal at family reunions, when my Mennonite cousins and aunts sit on the edge of the pool at the Bucks County Park, their prayer caps tucked under strapped white rubber swim caps. With her feet in the water, my mother takes the shape of a home-town mermaid, a renegade one—no dreamer—with short blond hair.

My mother is not a beauty, but what child knows? She has teeth I take care to watch when she laughs—an open-mouth rattled laugh that comes from the back of her throat. Her teeth snare that laugh and wrap it up like a gift, struggle it after a minute into a manageable smile. What softness she has is de-tachable—there is the softness of her hair, thick, dirty-blond, full of air; and the softness of her shoulders. She does nothing in the usual way to beautify herself, no lipstick or rouge, although she uses her eyes and turns of her head to draw attention away from her harshness. There is a ranging boniness to her face: she is jaw and nose and skull. But her face is tamed by her will, by discreet internal commands. She tries to be careful. She doesn't want me to think *animal* or *skull* or *creature* when I look at her. But I am her daughter, and that's what I think.

My mother cannot take her eyes away from the water. She stares straight out, past the breakers, to the dark line where the ocean diminishes, where it loses us. She talks to me, but I'm invisible, a fleck of her thinking. My nub of a brain works, works, and pitches across the summer air that separates us. She's ahead of me most of the time and she's tricky. Her eyes take on the dim blue or gray of the day's sky—whatever the day—reflective of light, unrevealing.

My mother is not the distinctly drawn mother of magazines; she is not clear-cut.

"If all of my loved ones were drowning," she says to me, to the me that is no one, "and I had the strength to save one—I'd save Ruth."

"You could save two," I say. But I know I am going under.

"I said if I could save *one*. Ruth is the luckiest woman I know. She'd be saved."

Ruth owns a beach house on Cape May. She doesn't farm. My mother says we will visit her sometime and sit on her glassed-in porch or step off her back steps and walk to the lighthouse. They know each other from high school, and they write to each other—they never call; they write long typed paragraphs. "News," my mother says when she tears the envelope open.

My mother favors lucky people, and that is a clear injustice she sets down before me as my special treat. "The lucky ones live, my darling. They have nothing to say about it, and they don't try."

"Am I lucky?"

"You may be. You're lucky to be a girl. Men are really unlucky; they have a hard time just living. Especially the powerful. They don't know what to do with the world, except run it."

"What does Ruth do?"

"Ruth? She does all kinds of things. We'll visit her sometime."

"What does she do?"

"I told you. You name it, she does it."

"Does she have a little girl?"

"No."

"Then aren't you lucky, too?"

"*Of course.* You know I'm lucky. I'm not going to drown—is that what you're thinking?"

I flounder, unrescued, whenever I try to step, like the footed farm child I am, stranger to beaches, afraid of the water that rolls and keeps rolling, pushing its last breakers like a fence toward me. The gentler lake of the sea must be somewhere out there, hedged, private. My mother is no help at all. She sends me off by myself, her fingertips cold on my shoulder: "Get your feet wet."

And she watches. I walk away to the wall of the ocean as it falls. I calculate how to touch the collapsing wall, how to tag it, and how to rush off within my own splashes, up the beach ahead of the foam and onto the dark sand that is colder than the spray of the waves.

My mother has me surrounded. I must be hers. Anyway, I am her daredevil. At the edge of the ocean, I wait for a wave to move in, and when a big one rolls over on its side and comes at me, I squint my eyes and watch until the last moment for her sake, and then like a baby sent to touch her fingertips to a dead body, experimentally—some verification of death that only a child, bounteous, could give with surety—in that child's wretched trembling for her own lively self, I touch the falling water with my fingers; then turn and run. Run toward my mother. Keeping ahead of the curve of foam. My toes spread apart in drier sand and I slow and slow. At her knees, I see my mother is looking beyond me, past the water. She's seeing the shells at the bottom of the sea, pearls on a murky platter.

I drop in the space beside her, which is first of all cool. I sit there, curled, her shell, right at hand. But after a time, the air turns feverish. Her warmth and the sun's warmth generate spirals, whirlwinds, around me, miraculously inside of me, and I sit up straight, extending my neck for cooler air.

My mother pulls me over; her hands catch the sides of my head. She draws my whole head down into her lap, my ears against her thighs. There is darkness and a surprising breeze between her legs, and she rubs my hair with her fingers. I feel grains of sand against my cheeks. Her motions are so sudden, consequences of rapid thoughts, which she doesn't disclose—her thoughts are all silence—and I am her hand-held charm. The strands of my hair, which she wraps around her fingers, are dry and hot and foreign; my hair belongs to some other child, a parched desert child.

My mother lifts my head. She holds my face toward the water.

"There's no end to it," she says, of the ocean, as if it could be said of nothing else in the world. My throat shuts; the air is dangerous. I fill with worry and it aches in my throat. There is nothing I will be able to prove to her. I see a short, handwritten letter: *I am here.* It would make her unhappy.

Soon my mother will go for another swim. To prepare myself, so I will not hold my breath the whole time, I imagine in careful detail my mother swimming the ocean, each ocean, out and out, swimming past channel buoys, past the last gulls; she swims the way doves fly, steadily, tirelessly, across the Atlantic and around the horn of Africa, Madagascar. A dot, she flurries a blue globe, tours like a minnow into Indian, Malaysian estuaries. Among strewings of islands, she swims the Pacific, curves with the equatorial waters, then dives to the south along the Chilean coast, colder and colder, through the sharp turn of the Strait of Magellan, and then warming with warm Atlantic currents, northward and northward. The waters are blue, aqua, translucent. She skims, glides, too far from Florida to be seen, up the Carolina coasts, slowing for Delaware. She could go on, but I always bring her back. She strokes to shore with the unvaried rhythm I have seen her practice in calm water. She swims very close to shore. I recognize her, the upswing of her chin, the O of her mouth, the rolling shoulders. Just beyond the breakers, she lets her legs fall under water, and she walks upright through the swells. On the beach, she brushes water down from her arms, down from her legs, and with quick shakes of her head, she spins her hair to the sides and walks to where I am in the sand, showering me.

I am warm and cold at the same time, however I think of her.

My mother lets go my head, and—there—I notice myself again,

in my own straight body, in my blue swimsuit a shade darker than hers. I push my fingers under the sand at my sides, and it covers them over, making a monster of me, fingerless, handless. I push under my feet. Imagine a child bounced on her torso along the beach, poor thing. That's me.

"You watch!" says my mother. "I'm riding those waves." And she lifts herself from the sand in one sidelong, thoughtless motion. She is halfway down the beach. I pull out my hands and feet—I'm whole—and up on my knees, I stretch my back to watch. She hits the water's edge and she slows all her motions. Even the water splaying out from her sides falls away stunned, whole droplets separate and distinct. Her fingertips touch the water, pull through it, and more finely visible disruptions occur. Then she sweeps herself up and over an incoming swell, momentarily gone. On the other side, she turns herself quickly around. Now a floater, she's swept and swept and lifted my way. Here she comes. I wave to greet her, my arrival. She waves once, her whole arm up, then down, and she turns away. She walks out, more slowly than before, farther through several breaking waves until she is deep in the water. She waits through a series of swells, lifting with them, and then with a large roll, she rises as if she would jump, horseback, whaleback, and she stretches her arms out and catches the building wave behind the cresting, its frilled mane there for her, and she rides, weightless again, headlong home. When the wave breaks and pulls back, my mother digs in her toes and leans to the beach, then rises against the undertow, against gravity, and stands up easily. She walks out of the water, shaking her head and flapping her arms. She kicks one leg out, stamps it in sand, kicks the other leg, too, and stamps. Her mouth hangs open and she walks toward me. At my side, she uses my head like a post to turn herself around; she kisses me, dripping water on top of my dry hair and dry shoulders, and then she falls down beside me.

"There! You should try that!" she says. Although she can see I am simply a toy, with no power of my own for covering the distance, no will of my own for joining forces.

"When can I try?" I ask.

"Float, first. We'll practice at home."

She might as well say to me, "Darling, fly. We'll practice when no one's looking."

"Have you tasted the salt?" my mother asks. "Here." She holds out her arm to me, the twist of muscle at the top of her forearm. "Taste it."

It is easy to do what my mother says. I lean over and with my mouth, which seems small now, and with my tongue, which is like a bird's tongue, short and stiff, I lick her arm. Twice. And push my tongue back and forth through my tight lips, scraping my teeth, sucking back the salt. I taste something that tastes like the sea, which may be the salt, but I feel on the tip of my tongue the trace of the hairs on her arm, a print of her sea-swimming arm. And I lick my own arm, which is a lifeless arm, elastic and flattened, not my own arm at all, not anyone's.

I have nothing that isn't hers.

"Salty," I say.

My mother sends me away, down the beach to meet my father and brother with their bucket full of black shells. I am her messenger and I run quickly to this man with the young man's face, who seems always just out of reach of my arms. I swoop by him, backtrack, and he does not catch me by the elbows or scoop me up, but bends down for a shell, blows the sand from it, and holds it out to me.

"Look at this one." He holds it by the side and I take the shell without touching his fingers.

"Mother's licking the salt off her arms," I tell him.

Then we're standing beside her.

"It's grainy," she explains.

"You're tasting it," my father says, "probably not feeling it."

This is how it goes. My mother leans back and straightens the shoulder of the arm she has licked, then she sticks out her whole tongue and licks again, largely.

"Salt dries," she insists. "I feel it. I feel the edges of crystals."

"It is not table salt on your arm. You imagine the crystals like salt on a radish." He is smiling, my father is, with his puff of brown hair and large brown mustache, like a boy in costume, acting up. "You taste salt, and you no doubt think table salt, and you most likely think of the salt on a radish."

"Ha," says my mother.

Ha, I say to myself. She wouldn't think salt on a radish any more than a fish would think of its salty waters as table salt melted in rain. A child knows it. I know it.

"The angles of crystals," my father goes on, "are microscopic. It's unlikely a human tongue could appreciate them as edges."

"Unlikely?" My mother decides they will stop here. She looks at me: I'm a punctuation mark.

"Unlikely." He sees it coming, but cannot in good conscience omit the qualifier. "I'd say close to impossible."

"Close to impossible," my mother concludes, as she likes to conclude, with the possible in her favor.

Isn't It Something?

This is how Celia told it.

Her ex-husband loved her maiden name, Dollop—so much that he said keep it, you keep it, when they married. He said, you are Celia Dollop and that is who. She told him it was a stupid, lopsided name, but he said no, it was rich, a home-baked name, full of goodies and promise. Yum, he said, and he did his nibbling. For a while. But sooner than she'd dreamed, Celia Dollop was walking herself to Mercy Hospital with a broken collarbone and an index finger pointing backwards, and that night she swore on the Bible in the gray metal drawer that she'd vacate the state. Again. For good. With fifty dollars in her coat from the Mercy Female Crisis Fund, Celia Dollop signed herself out and got a Gray Lady to drive her across the border into Lenawee County, the edge of Michigan, where Celia's uncle Lee had an empty house on some property he used for hunting. She broke in through a back window. She said her uncle would be glad to have the house occupied.

This is the house where I met Celia, and around that house, in that vicinity, is the only place I ever saw her. The house was a white box that sat in the open just beyond a turn in Culbert Road, a gravel road with swamps falling away on either side. My girls and I usually saw wood ducks in those swamps, and we walked there, with binoculars, on weekends during the late spring and early summer. Celia noticed us walking on the road one morning and invited us in for lemonade. She and I sat on her back porch, a cement slab that was crumbling away from all of the rock salt she must have poured on it through the winter. We sat in the sun and we watched my girls climb an apple tree, in full blossom, the only tree in her yard. There were bees buzzing in most of the flowers, but the girls didn't mind, and, for them, the noisy, sweet canopy was something special. Celia brought me a plastic glass of lemonade, gave me a newspaper to sit on, and in every way treated me like a child. I was probably a couple of years older than she was.

She wore a green sundress and green plastic flip-flops. Celia was large, but not weighty; her flesh was an unmuscled, malnourished flesh, the kind that swings on the bone. When I think of her, I think of profusions of flesh—her legs, from her knees to her ankles, thick and soft; her arms, shoulders to elbows, pale pink. She looked malleable, like something refrigerated, sweetly doughy. On her arms and legs, hardly noticeable, grew fine blond hair. Her face was round, but her features were usually hidden by long glossy auburn curls, which may have been one of K Mart's better wigs. I'd have had to touch it to know for sure.

From the first, I liked to listen to Celia's voice, mild and careening. Sometimes she'd lean close, go whispery, and then lean away to build up to a low-pitched laugh that came out like a cough. It was a rocking, lullaby voice. She told me her name, which I, too, admired, and she told me the story of her marriage and how her name figured in that. It was restful listening to her. She talked about her past as if it were long gone, a baby's life, in another country or another climate, a poor place with brutal men. She mentioned that she was completely healed; that it was heaven here on a gravel road, living alone. Her ex-husband had moved to Dayton. "Dayton!" she said. It made sense to her. "He doesn't write," Celia said. She stretched her arms out as if she were yawning, and the puffs of flesh behind her elbows swayed like hammocks. "More lemonade?"

"Sure," I said.

We both stood to go into the kitchen, and I held the screen door for her. It was dark inside. Celia had spread newspapers on the floor after washing it, and the room rattled when we walked.

"My cousin Joseph, in Reno," Celia said, "was the one I called the first time I had to get out of Ohio." She pulled a round box of instant lemonade out of the cupboard. "I left in a hurry. Never stay," she said, "when a man goes wild."

I sat in a wooden chair by the square wooden table in the middle of the room. The kitchen had nothing in it but the table, two chairs, a porcelain sink standing on two metal legs—the crook of the drainpipe wrapped with insulation—and a two-door cupboard to the left of the sink. If she had a stove and a refrigerator, they were in another room. In the months I knew her, I never saw her cook, or eat. Right up to the end, I thought she lived on peace and quiet. There was a small window, high up, over the sink; it was curtained with green material and very little light came through. Even in daytime, Celia turned on the ceiling light, a fixture with unshaded bulbs, and the room flashed gray to the corners: the walls gray-papered, the floor gray linoleum and coated with damp, graying newspapers.

Celia stirred my lemonade with a long-handled spoon. "My cousin Joseph could have been a twin. I'd heard about him, as a kid, but we'd never met. At the bus station we shook hands, and then we kissed. I tell you, sweetie, we were lovers from hello. When he died, it wasn't the sadness you'd think. It was leukemia—anyway, it was fast, like a thing disappearing out of nature. Something endangered. Extinct. *That* was the day I should have gone into solitary."

"This is solitary?"

"Look around," she said. She showed off the room with a pleasure that lowered her shoulders and made her sigh. "It's the other side of the world. I remembered this place from when I was little, coming here with my dad and my uncle Lee when they hunted the Basso. I slept on the cot in the next room. They sat out here playing cards, and the kerosene lamp sent a yellow cone of light over their hands. I'd lie with my eye to the wallboards, and I could see through a crack to watch them, and listen. They didn't talk much, but they sat in the lamplight and snapped cards, as easy and natural as if *that* was the only life there was. Just that—quiet. Some shadows."

"You got a car?"

"No means of transportation," she said. "None." She was proud of it.

I sucked on the lemonade. Peaceful descriptions, pastoral scenes, make me nervous; I've never experienced peace in my life, and I don't want to. I don't trust the idea. I keep my car running— that's why I work, and that's where my money goes. I should have said so then. But if Celia wanted peace, this was the place. Her yard adjoined the Basso Game Area, a state park with nothing in it but two gravel roads, weeds, and a three-fingered lake.

"I'm pleased to be here," Celia said, and it sounded like a conclusion. She stood up, her curls parting down the middle of her forehead, and I saw a scar that nearly closed one eye. She held the door for me, and we went outside.

My girls were stepping, one limb to the next, in the middle level of the tree; it was hard to tell which one was following, which one leading. Celia and I sat on the cement slab, our feet in the driveway, and watched them circling. I told Celia where I lived, and I mentioned Harry. I don't talk much to my family, even less to friends.

"He isn't the father of my girls," I told her, "but he's a good father." That's about all I said.

"Is he good to you?" She meant did he beat me.

"It's rough sometimes."

"Sweetie, just leave," she said. "It's like this. You take the suitcase out of the closet, you pack it up. You call a friend, anyplace. You say, well, I'm on my way. Say, oh, not for long. You get money for bus tickets, no more. And you go. Don't plan. —Not that branch, honey," she called to my youngest daughter. "You can think on the bus. Tell me one good thing that was planned."

I couldn't think, offhand.

"So, you plan on the bus. That's why you take the bus. What I tell you about buses," Celia said, hushing her voice, "you must believe. But don't let it stop you." She brushed an ant off my shoe.

"What about buses?"

"Well, keep a handbag in your lap. Pay some attention, or somebody making a getaway out of Dayton will slip his hand between your legs when you're falling to sleep. I clamped a man," she said, "red-handed. He sat beside me, out of Dayton, a perfect stranger, ho hum, not a word, and then when I blink one minute off to sleep, pitter pitter patter, he gets right to business looking for comfort. This was Columbus to Reno. I clamped him there and I said, do I yell *fire* or do you move off, and forever? He was mild-mannered enough. He saw how things were. But that was the bus that took me to Reno." Celia's shoulders relaxed; her arms settled across her lap. She'd swung herself back to a point of calm, where it seemed she could quit.

"I've never been west," I said.

"Well, go. It is very brown and airy out there. In a couple of days, you almost forget how hard it is to breathe anywhere else. But you see the cactus plants, you see everything shut up and storing water, and it's a reminder. I met the gentlest men you could dream of," Celia said. "I couldn't believe it. I've wondered since, though, if they were that way before they went to Reno. Maybe it's the desert. When you sleep in the desert, you soften. Well, at night the muslin sheets were cool and you could lie there talking until it was dark and only the sheets caught some light. I never knew anything like it," Celia said.

"It sounds nice."

"Take a bus," she said.

"I got a car. But it's not that simple." I got up and walked toward the apple tree. I knew peace of mind when I saw it, and it always made me fidget. She'd saved herself; she'd been converted.

"It's simple. Pay attention," she said.

Without looking around, I could tell she was straightening her shoulders, pulling herself up. To match her, I pushed back my shoulders and stretched up my hand. I heard a couple of vertebrae in my neck crack. "Let's walk through the Basso," I called over my shoulder.

"I'll get my shoes." Celia kicked off her flip-flops there in the driveway and went in the house. Then an arm reached out, and she set a large spray can outside the door; she bent herself out of the door, on one leg; her whole body leaned over; one hand held the doorknob. "Here's some Off for the girls." Then she swayed back into the dark.

"We're going through the Basso," I called to my girls, who came running from either side of the tree trunk, screaming, "Yay!" They passed the Off can back and forth. Holding their eyes shut with their hands, each sprayed the other, in great clouds, front and back.

Celia came out, with heavy walking boots on, no visible socks. I set my lemonade in the grass, and the four of us walked across her back yard, through a border of high weeds and into the flatland scrub of the Basso. My girls ran ahead, pulling goatsbeard out by the root, squeezing bunches, and blowing away the huge puffs like enormous dandelions in the wind.

"Some people, muddle them as you want," Celia said, "set in this field, they could tell you the day of the month by what's blooming. Some species—this," she picked a low-lying pink flower, "are so short-lived."

"Too bad they don't last," I said.

"Nonsense. It's a good thing," she said, and she tossed the flower away.

Celia wanted an argument, but I put up my binoculars and spotted some field sparrows and bobolinks and, in the new locusts, cedar waxwings. Celia glanced at the birds when I pointed them out, but just as a favor. She kept her eye out for wildflowers, not much else. She walked with her head down, scanning the weeds. Along a dirt roadway, she bent down in her odd bird-bend, one-footed, to pick several short stalks with three or four spiky purple flowers climbing the stems. There were more patches of the flowers, edging the road, as we walked. "These like sterile soils," she told me. She picked two handfuls. "*Specularia perfoliata.*"

The road gradually sloped toward the lake, and before long we could see the blue water up ahead. The girls were already there, peeling off their shoes and socks, leaning against each other and hopping around. When Celia and I got to where they'd been, the girls were waving to us from a large flat rock offshore. "An island!" they yelled and pointed down.

Celia took a crumpled paper towel from the pocket of her sundress and dipped it in the lake, wrung it out, and wrapped it around the stalks of the wildflowers, in two bouquets. "By the end of June," she said, "you won't find much else here. They love poor ground." When my girls splashed in to shore, I thought Celia was going to offer them the flowers, but she kept the bouquets for herself, one in each fist.

Going back, Celia led us a different way, through a dried-up swamp with a peat bed, black and cushiony. The girls jumped on it, bending their knees like gymnasts, pretending it was more than it was.

"Don't you go out?" I asked Celia. We crossed the last hedge-row and pushed through the highest weeds back toward her yard.

"I do not!"

I told her I had the car if she needed anything. Or if she wanted to go somewhere. I told her that I worked, and that I took some courses in Adrian at night, if she wanted to come.

"You are looking at a homebody," Celia Dollop said.

"You're deprived," I said. It's one thing I said.

"That's what I mean, thank you," Celia said. "I'm down to nothing; it's about time."

Back at the house, Celia sat on the cement to undo her boots. She didn't wear socks. She asked my girls to bring her the flip-flops, and then she sat there, her hands shading her eyes, saying good-bye to us, saying stop in the next time we were out walking, she'd be around.

Harry said leave her alone if that's what she wanted. But the girls and I took a few walks the next weekends anyway, and stopped in to see Celia Dollop four or five times. I took her newspapers: I knew she could use them for her floors, if she didn't read them, and she was appreciative. It's hard to imagine a person in the Northern Hemisphere living with less. Celia grew two tomato plants by her back door; I noticed those. And once she took a letter out of her mailbox while I was there. She showed no interest in it, although it was handwritten, in red ink, and addressed to her. My guess is she never read it.

Since I work days, I can't be sure that Celia didn't get around. Maybe her uncle Lee brought food, or took her to town. I don't have the evidence. I saw her a few Saturday afternoons, inside and outside her house, and it was always the same: we drank lemonade, she did the talking, and we went walking.

And then I didn't see her any more. Ever.

She was murdered. The way murders happen outside of small towns. A crazed man comes out of the past, and tears a woman apart. He kills her children, if she's got any. But Celia didn't.

That's all I can say. I haven't said much to Harry.

The only one I really want to talk to about it is Celia. Isn't it something?

I never really talked to her; she didn't know one thing about me except that I was afraid, and afraid to talk. But she was working on me. I'd have come around.

I don't know much else about Celia Dollop. With so many people, all that you ever know is their talk. When they're gone, it's finished.

Yesterday I told my girls. I told them, if somebody interesting talks to you, you say a few things, too. You might as well breathe at the same time and let the words out in the air. Don't just ask questions, I told them. Give things away. Give yourself away.

They stood there, listening. They listen to me.

Who Has Lived from a
Child with Chickens

Hester, Melissa, and Colleen were the three chickens who turned everything around, who ended the reign of Ratzafratz the Fat—our Razzie, our Raz—and who restored as nearly as possible the Age of Egg, with its routine perfections and disproportions in form and taste. An egg is no sphere; and this is no tale of sentiment; it's no *Animal Farm* with sides to jump to or enemies to chuck. A sequence of events occurred. Simply. The way things do.

Queen for an episode or two was Colleen, the usual dullard; Hester and Melissa attended, dotingly. I am talking about Colleen the Chicken, a commonplace Rhode Island Red with typically underdeveloped comb. Unlike Hester and Melissa, Colleen was named for a person, a sweet-faced college freshman who sat weightlessly in a front-row seat in my General Civ class—a guileless, guiltless child who still wrote, in 1973, letters to the student paper chastising the school's cheerleaders for their slumping and scowling at games; she knew by instinct the traditional rules of conduct and experienced what appeared to be allergenic reactions to breaches of such codes. She had blue eyes, always misted as if by a mysterious makeup. Colleen the Chicken resembled Colleen the Child not at all, but when Colleen Chicken scuffed her way under the wire fence for the third time and the kids said, "Hey, let's name the one that always gets out!" I naturally said, "Why not?" It was my turn to name. Hester and Melissa were Robbie and Cy's picks, names yanked from the air. They were chickens with no heritage.

The tunneling hen didn't remind me of anybody; she was molting, still more chick than hen. I stood, stumped, at the wire fence, bending it up for the chicken to crawl back. "No name. I give up."

Robbie was five, Marine-square.

"All right," he said, "give me the first name that comes to your head."

"Colleen."

The syllables were there: wide and shining and imprecise. It felt like a reflex, a throwback, this recollection of Colleen, her wide milkface, the slightly crooked nose, her wool sweaters and long bland curls. The only time I heard her speak, she complained to a friend about the awful humidity frizzing her hair. Her voice was not unpleasant, and her hair, I decided then, was her fairest feature. So Colleen it was. And was to be. Not Joyce, the freckled, promiscuous, lyrical; not Sue, the muscled swimmer who lived like a hermit and ate only Cheez-its; not Rosemary Dunlap (Dr. Dunlap) who lived upstairs on our Dorchester Street place and had screaming fits on her latticed sunporch. Colleen was the one who floated up first, a breathy balloon.

. . .

The three years that Razzie held sway in the goat shed were years of drought, tornado, and freeze. Weeds flourished and bloomed lustily while the eggplants stood stunted, skeletal, each with its four yellow leaves. Aphids ate everything decorative, including a hedgerow of hardy multiflora. A tornado lifted a trailer down the road and dropped a doorknob on our driveway. We knew it was a plague—there is always one plague or another—but we had no idea, understandably, that Razzie the Fat was implicated. At first, we (me and Hazard, my husband) worried that, as for the eggplants, our applications of mulch were to blame, that the walnut leaves mixed with the oak may not have been acid enough. Or worse, that the goat manure we spread on the north side had leached to the south in irregular patterns and we'd planted the eggplants in the barren spots. Who could tell? I reread the Eggplant entry in the *Encyclopedia of Organic Gardening*, but found no clues. As for the aphids, I knew we had ladybugs, but not enough. It takes thousands. After the first year of devastation, I'd introduced into the coldframe a few stray ladybugs we'd found trapped between windows and storm windows in the house. My plan was to breed a horde of them to help out during the July aphid ravage. The ladybugs seemed content in the coldframe, and I thought the first week I spotted some extras. Then they disappeared. We gave up on the multiflora by late August, and they stood through the fall like winter shrubs along the boundary line. Even so, we might not have suspected an unnatural, localized plague if other things hadn't happened. For instance, the jasmine thistles.

Brittle, red-flowering thistles grew in the lawn, not just in patches, but in wide, circling swaths, which sometimes changed directions overnight. Their perfume, disorienting as fog, rose from the flowers and drifted with the motions of the plants. It was impossible to walk barefoot outside. Sneakers with socks were insufficient; the thistly spines grew luxuriantly and needled through to the ankles even though the grass was new-cut. The *Field Guide to Wildflowers* included no red-flowering thistles (ours flowered every day, flat to the ground, five-petaled, blood-red). Robbie and Cy wore long pants and high shoes for those two summers, and I finally drove to S & H for a pair of heavy-duty work boots.

After meals, I sat on the porch with my nose in a cup of cold coffee, my feet propped on the metal railing, and I remembered my great-grandmother who stirred a brew of witch hazel and barks with a hand-hammered iron spoon. I remembered a painting in the Art section of *Time* magazine of a woman on a straw prairie under an umbrella, alone and content, maybe falling asleep.

Hazard had the idea he could harvest the thistle flowers and make a sweet wine, like dandelion wine. Wearing winter gloves, he filled two brown paper bags with blossoms. "Nipped in the bud," he said on his way into the house. One night, he stepped through the bedroom door, one naked half of his body after the other, a glass of red-thistle wine in each hand. "It's perfume," he said. "For you!" And he tipped one glass, like a government official, over my head. "For me!" he said. With the other glass, he doused himself. To celebrate one more disordered fact of life, we made suffocating, jasmine love at the foot end of the bed. Part of the time, we held our noses.

Still, each winter, the thistles frosted, turned black, and died like everything else. We took heart. Winter froze what it could, and that seemed appropriate. Cold we could handle. Hazard and I decided, by January, that the summer had not really been disastrous or terrifying at all. It had been cooked up.

In the shed, Ratzafratz, too, cooled off through the winter. He made himself scarce, touring his complex of tunnels under the hay and manure in the goat stalls, and continuing on through the wallboard to the chicken room of the shed, then flat along the cement-block wall where the straw was kicked up, cushy. Every three weeks on Saturday I cleaned the shed, down to the concrete, and heaped the dark forkloads of manure onto mounds that steamed west of the barn. With all of the shed doors open, Hester, Melissa, and Colleen followed me around, snapping up the small green alfalfa leaves and the spare cuts of corn. Always we watched out for Raz, who was obese and distinguishable from any other rat by his girth, and by a black mask, raccoonlike, slipped over his nose. But in spite of his weight, he was slick, very fast, and he slipped by us, while the rest of his pack was methodically, unhysterically, done in. His was a life of disappearances, rejuvenations, mysteries.

To clean the shed, I used a straight-pronged garden fork, not a wispy pitchfork for those laden hauls. A garden fork is a murderous tool. In essence and function, it is four primitive iron knives. When I got a rat with that fork, I got it twice. Hester, Melissa, and Colleen went for the eyes, and death was quick, decisive. I'd set my S & H boot on the body, pull back the fork, sweep the limp soul up and lift it outside, and swing wide around, pitching it far into the burdock for the buzzards. More ecological than D-Con pellets. No blood, no rot.

But Raz, by fishlike maneuvering and underworld trampolining, was two feet ahead of the fork, even when I stabbed four feet ahead in the tunnel. Sometimes I'd see a tail, snapping away, or, turning a forkful of hay, I'd see the swatchy black nose at the disrupted end of the tunnel, just for a blink. Then he'd suck himself back, probably turn or roll over according to incomprehensible rat-body law, and be safe, breathing slowly, in the corner of the chicken room before I could pull back my arm in javelin form to throw the fork. He could always relax, kinglike, somewhere in his maze; longevity alone is a solid base of power.

I knew he'd done serious damage in the shed, gnawing good wood and probably scaring the milk from Emma Peel's udder the one night I went out and found her sitting, stricken, in the ridiculous way goats can sit, like teen-agers with long arms dangling, not a drop of milk in her, for no reason. The rat could be petty. Colleen, loose from her room, was beside Emma that night, pacing, clucking a low muttering cluck. Ratzafratz may have gone bodily through the plasterboard wall of the chicken room; I discovered a wide tear, with six inches of chalky board crumbling and hanging loose. Colleen could have, must have, walked right through.

Colleen was beginning to approximate the attitudes of her namesake, looking blandly, judgmentally at me—things were not as they should be. Definitely not, in her eyes, as they should be.

From the night she appeared at Emma Peel's side, Colleen assumed an authority in the shed that surprised us all, walking around in the center of things, leading Hester and Melissa down the slide in the morning, scratching up the first sow bug. In the past, she'd been a malingerer, really, sometimes just perching dreamily at the edge of the nest boxes, eating casually without any flutter, sometimes not going outside all day. She'd laid large eggs, without any of the usual fuss.

But through that last winter, she began building up a good fluff of feathers; the red skin spots she used to peck and rub open were gradually filled out with soft, small, hairlike feathers, and these then were covered, layered, with the flat red, overlapped look of healthy Rhode Island feathering. There were tufts, almost epaulets, on her shoulders, and her tail was an alert comprehensive fan.

By spring Hester and Melissa were shaping up, too. The three, when they walked around the bare chicken yard, picked up their feet and stepped in full-length strides. They turned in file, the inside one pivoting with real precision, the others lengthening their steps, circling around. I didn't mention their exercises to anybody; in fact, I pretended not to notice, and just looked sidelong at the drills while I pinched the Japanese beetles off the Chinese elm. But one day Cy yelled from the porch, "The chickens are marching!" Thereafter their habits became a subject for family discussion, Hazard pointing out to the children that chickens were just chickens. "But, evidently," I carped back, "weather is no longer weather, nor nature, nature."

Of some interest to me, who has lived from a child with chickens, was the alteration in Colleen's comb—it was still small, as hens' combs are, but it glistened, took on a bluish cast, very much like the sudden paling, the blanching to blue, that occurs at chicken death. When a dog hits a chicken, one knows by the comb how bad it is, and if there's hope. But Colleen's comb both blued and flourished; she looked better than ever. She looked strong, like a WAC.

I was glad to see something that hinted of strength and good circulation—it hadn't rained once in April, just a light drizzle on May Day, and the rest of May withered on, wilting. The *Almanac*, once again, was all lies. We watered the coldframe, but the seedlings were giving away moisture to air; their stems would fall flat on the sand—I could see the vermiculite lumps right through them—by late afternoon. The garden lay yellow and dry, loose as a beach, down a foot, and there it would turn into hardpan, packed solid as boards. Our lawn never greened, although the red-petaled thistles were coming on strong.

June the first, having no garden, no grass, nothing to worry about losing, I decided to let the chickens out of their yard, to scratch at will.

Colleen stepped out first, Melissa and Hester in line behind, four and a half paces apart. With some fancy footwork, Colleen and the others surrounded the first thistle plant they came to, and, in precisely coordinated fashion, pecked it to pieces, red flowers going down last, little pompoms in beaks.

Robbie said, "Wow."

I thought, There's a plan here. Intuitive rigor. They move by design. But I said, "Yeah."

The face of Colleen the Child floated back, her brows set; she'd approve of these chickens—they figured things out with their flat circly eyes, saw a job, and got at it. It was easy to do what had to be done, and they had the gizzard to do it. Eat thistles. I felt humble, glad I'd acknowledged their talents, their taste. During the weeks of scooping cracked cornmeal into their feeder, I'd noticed with discomfort how the feed bags puffed a dry dust into my nose, and I'd thought how the chickens must suffer, the tiny holes of their beaks stuffing up, their feathers filling with dry small flakes from the kernels. I'd done the right thing finally opening their gate and giving them greenery, good juices.

That afternoon, while I was holding a hose on a three-foot pear tree, Robbie tore around the corner of the house, his whole body leaning, boots nearly sliding from under him, yelling, "Colleen's got a rat! Cornered!"

"Raz?"

"I don't know. Big as a groundhog."

"That's him!" And I was halfway around the house. "Get the fork!"

When I hit the path to the shed, I could see Colleen, her wings flung back in her most militant stance; she was side-stepping a definite half-circle in one corner of the yard, back and forth, solid and fierce, with Hester and Melissa behind her on either side, backing her up. Ratzafratz it was—in the corner, up on his hind legs, as wide as he was high, his two teeth out like an armored bib, his bent, black-wire claws stabbing ping ping ping toward Colleen, his motions stirring up heat waves out through the yard.

"Where's the fork?" I screamed at Robbie, who didn't budge

at the back porch. Colleen glanced in my direction, giving me the go-ahead. I had to shrug, empty-handed. When we both looked back at Ratzafratz, he'd converted himself to empty space. The air spread out, absolutely still. A clean, perfect getaway.

She'd done more than her part, getting him out in broad daylight, out in the open yard. I was astonished at her commitment to duty, a duty beyond her realm, to my mind. If she'd scratched out a letter to Senator Plampin and complained about road crews pulling up bittersweet, endangered as it was, I wouldn't have been more impressed. Here was a blatant abuse confronted forthwith, forthright. Thoughtlessly. Colleen had no understanding of moments, of lapses. Razzie may also have turned in his mind the matter of Colleen's nerve. I'm sure he had not anticipated her moves.

That evening—as the TV predicted: it was no surprise—the weather switched: the vacant clear skies of two months were sucked eastward in a vacuumlike wind, and huge rolls of black and gray-green clouds tumbled in from the west. There were hours of dusk as the doomy underbellies of storm clouds trapped a steady, dim light. Tornado watches were posted and I knew we were in for it. By the time Hazard got home, the evening had turned into a heavy, noisy blackness, and we carried the radio and flashlights into the basement, took a pop-up book for the kids, some beers, and old blankets for the cold floor.

I felt better than usual about the animals, nature back in season as it seemed to be. I didn't worry much until one blast of wind and sledge-hammering thunder took out the electricity, and in the first pause after that blow I thought I heard Emma Peel baa her high whinnying baa. But, with a couple of hours until morning, I just shut my ears, let the house shudder, and imagined myself like Razzie, wedged in a tunnel, Colleen nearby with her dull eyes open, everything blowing over.

After a storm it's never easy to take the first look around, but this time I was upstairs in the kitchen and out the back door with the earliest light. Wind was still thumping the windowpanes roped to the coldframe and whishing hard across the back yard, whipping thistles. I could see the shed, in solid outline. Closer, slight damage—the front door, never quite straight, was pulled from one hinge, tipped out and wide open; some shingles were torn, some gone; the big window in the chicken room was cracked across. Colleen was standing in the open door, triumphant, I thought—no, shoulders back slightly, appropriately, her simple greeting.

She stepped aside according to antique protocol, then she turned and walked into the chicken room and hopped in her nest box. She was back on schedule. I walked ahead to the goat stalls, where Emma and Shy Violet blinked at me, head-on, emptily. The old diehard look. Somewhere behind a wall Melissa and Hester scratched and clucked indifferently, just as they had in bygone days, not minding Colleen.

I went back to the chicken room to check out Colleen, and I saw them, both of them: Colleen with her old-fashioned slump, squatting dreamy-eyed there in her box, egg laid, the blank calm of her life returned; and off to the side, Ratzafratz, flat on his back, already stiff, near the feeder, his claws skimpy, hooked into nothing.

I checked him over for blood, wounds—the chickens had got at his eyes, but otherwise he looked clean. "Hmm. Colleen." I looked her in the eye, but she stared back at me from far off in chickenworld, flat-eyed, unblinking, not hiding anything. A shadow wavered across her beak—no, not a shadow, some dark hairs. I looked back at Razzie, then picked up a stiff weed out of the straw and used it to lift the hairs at his neck. Colleen would go for the jugular. She'd been through training.

The straw in that corner of the room was scruffed in a triangle, the same lines I'd seen in the chicken yard. I don't think the wind could have done it. I've never read in the *How to Raise Pullets* pamphlets anything comprehensive about chicken-scratch patterns, or tactics and attitudes of defense. Somebody should write these things down.

Predictably, after that night of storm it rained for three days, consolingly, the kind of rain that could help Ratzafratz to his colorful, chemical decay.

We buried him out on the boundary line, between two bare multiflora stalks, having determined, in council, that his was a passing worthy of ceremony.

Colleen didn't notice the funeral in the rain; it was very simple— we put him in a hole and covered him up.

This summer, as should be the case in temperate zones, the garden is growing and the redroots, naturally, are shading out carrots and celery. The ordinary scene. The daily trouble. I've no complaints. Melissa, Hester, and Colleen wiped out the this- tles in the yard, and all three are molting again, as they should. I still clean the shed every three weeks, fork rats when I must.

These days of drifting July heat, I've wondered sometimes if Colleen from college ever figured a way to embrace the humid, swirling hemisphere that messed her hair. She probably still wears campus coordinates, still knows precisely what she thinks. I imag- ine her fierce, decorous, dull. But in these years of unaccountable catastrophe and rescue, I've learned—let's see—the generosity of fair report. And as far as Colleen goes, Chicken or Child, I simply give credit where credit is due.

Patriotic

Jesus, this is hard on me," says Floyd Dey.

He hooks a hay bale out of the chute and lifts it in front of him the way he would lift a girl cousin. He carries the hay, maybe sixty pounds, to the back of the wagon. There he starts a second tier, up and over, rolling the bale once—there it is.

After an hour's work on a hay wagon with a seventeen-year-old kid, who is shirtless and scratching his navel, I myself quit complaining. This isn't labor. If it's hot, I twist the sleeves of my T-shirt up on my shoulders in doughy rolls, and I say to myself, okay.

To be fair, Floyd doesn't take the work seriously. But he knows what looks good—and for his own sake, he fakes the complaint. And he leans his back, the long tan of it, against the hay to relax. His two dark tits, flat as stickers, face my way. Floyd is hairless.

He seems to understand, his demeanor demonstrates that he understands—like the Oriental masterminds of pain who settle their bare skins down on steel spikes—how a grain of tolerance can look like bliss.

I take the next bale and hike it up against my hipbone. Floyd waits his turn, visibly at rest, involved in the dynamics of vertical pause. Once in a while, he closes his eyes. It has come and gone from Floyd's attention that under my V-neck shirt my breasts are smallish pegs, with nubbed blueberry nipples.

I don't wear a bra to bale—it would fill with leaves.

Maybe Floyd blinks at me. It is not discernible.

Floyd is a neighbor; he helps me out. Breezy, hay-drying days, my husband works, hammering at barn roofs and stapling together pre-fab constructions, across two counties. Sheds, garages go up overnight. It's seasonal work, which keeps him away from the sunny fields, and I find my own help.

Over the years, I've learned what to look for.

Floyd Dey is a high-school senior. I don't call him *boy* to his face; he never says *crone*. In other words, Floyd Dey and I get along. After three years, three cuttings of hay a year, we have fair-weather days down pat. I do this; he does that. Nobody shirks. Floyd Dey, by any measure, rates as goodhearted. When Floyd talks to me, he looks me straight in the eye.

He's the middle of three brothers, the only one blessed with the talent of health. Eugene, the older one, took a job this year with a mining company in Utah: a sour, sharp-witted boy who doesn't like sharing work and doesn't like rest. The youngest brother, Harry T., programmed a computer this year, Floyd says, with crop variables—soil types, seeds, moisture, fertility—and predicted the yields in several DeKalb test plots. Harry T. is thirteen. If he's strong enough to help next year, I'll probably find his facts useful.

"Floyd," I say, "I appreciate the fact that you look me in the eye."

"No foolin," he says, looking at me. "You're an appreciative person."

I am that. I am also thin, stripped with muscle, a Democrat.

For his birthday, Floyd bought a green-and-flesh '57 Ford, which he drives with care and which he always parks under the plum tree near the barn. Today, the second day of baling, he lifts himself out of the car, into the speckled shade, and right there pulls his T-shirt out from his jeans and peels it up like a skin over the top of his head. Then he slams the car door.

"Yo!" he calls on his way across the yard. He leaps, right foot up on the tongue of the hay wagon, left foot up on the flatbed. Here he kicks at the mounds of green and yellowing alfalfa dust from yesterday, and in that cloud he makes his way to the back latticework of two-by-fours that brace the bales.

It's the step of a man making himself at home.

He tosses his T-shirt up like a cap. The shirt snags where he wants it, on top of an upright, and a hot, cooperating wind lifts it dreamily.

Flag's up. The kid is ready to sail.

In the kitchen, I am on the phone with Mrs. Bagnoli, who in this lurch, in this perpetual lack of the able-bodied, I call on to help as tractor driver. I've heard about her; I've read her name in the papers.

"This is a Ford 4000," I say. "You know it?"

She plowed, she insists, in her springtimes in Oscoda, and last summer, when her nephew Rodney crushed himself under his Ford 4000 in mud, she was the one to bring some boards and the CPR people, and drive the sullied tractor home. Rodney's still saying thanks.

"I know the 4000," she swears. "I know it clean through."

Mrs. Bagnoli is also known to me as the woman whose husband survived eight hours in a moving cement mixer. I would never have thought it possible for a man to hang on, if what he did was hang on, or walk against the rotation, if he did walk against the rotation.

Although Mrs. Bagnoli lives on a farm three miles away, we have talked only a few times on the phone. She tells me her husband works at the Ford plant in Saline; *she* is the one who drives their wide-wheeled John Deere diesel.

"I'm on my way," she insists. "Glad to help. Happy to."

Through the screen door, I can see the hay wagon hitched in back of the red International 420 baler, and the blue Ford tractor in front. Seeing that display, seeing Floyd—like my own son on a flag-waving wagon, allowing the wind to mess his long hair—I decide that this is a day I could call myself—what is it?—patriotic? When the back of the neck is cool; the palms of the hands, tropical?

"Well, then," I say to Mrs. Bagnoli on the phone. "See you."

I fill a wide-mouthed jug with water and ice cubes, and cap it. From a shelf, I take the black hay hook, and halfway out the door, I reach back to the Kleenex box and stuff my pockets with yellow tissues.

Floyd is not one to carry Kleenex, even though his nostrils collect a leafy debris—even though he seems to enjoy making noises blowing his nose. I have told Floyd that Kleenex serves a working function, too. If the hay turns damp or wads up with weeds, we twist scraps of Kleenex as markers under the twine of wet bales.

In the barn, I set the wet bales aside. Floyd cooperates in these precautions, although he claims he has never seen steamy bales. "It happens," I say. "Spontaneous combustion."

Disaster has a cause, I try to tell him.

· · ·

I cross the driveway, and I whistle the "Marseillaise" as far as I know it. When the tune gives out, I start again, mumbling the words that Floyd might or might not know in French. *Allons, enfants de la patrie. . . .*

Up on the wagon, Floyd, who is placid, always in the present moment, turns when he hears me. He stands, cross-armed, massaging both his shoulders. I greet him in sunlight that casts a bluish-gold sheen on every surface. It looks like the sun on the sea, like the sun in Hawaii on T.V.

"What luck," I say.

I swing a landowner's arm around, palm up.

From the wagon, Floyd surveys the landscape. What he sees are low, aquamarine hills of alfalfa, steep slopes, and gravelly glacial dumps with swamps in the sockets. Above it all, the sky is blue, top to bottom.

"You order this day?" he asks.

With the tips of his fingers, he rubs his belly lightly, using both hands, back and forth, along the line of his lower ribs.

A boy is not to be blamed for thoughtlessness.

I check twine; I push dust from the knotters; I count the shear pins glittering in the tool box.

Down the driveway, a black Chevy pickup rolls in and roars its engine. The driver downshifts twice and gravel smacks the siding of the house.

"Wild," says Floyd.

He jumps from the wagon to help me tighten the tension on the baler. We take the threaded handles either side of the chute, and we wind them down.

Mrs. Bagnoli drives the pickup, too fast, in the general direction of the barn. She runs off the driveway and cuts through the yard, aiming the grille right at us. I see her head, low in the cab, and her elbow out the driver's window. But I can't see where she's looking.

Floyd and I both take one step back.

At the last minute, the pickup veers, sharp to the left, toward the tractor, and Mrs. Bagnoli must pull the truck's emergency brake and smash the foot brake simultaneously, because the truck skids a couple of inches and stops, one tire kissing the tread of the tractor's rear tire. Mrs. Bagnoli pitches herself into the steering column. I see a twist of gray hair against the windshield.

"Jesus," says Floyd.

He takes in a breath and holds it. I don't notice what I do.

But Mrs. Bagnoli appears unharmed. With a motion that has to be called bobbing, she drops herself out of the truck, goes around the back end, and comes at us with a smile.

"It is *criminal*," she says, in a festive voice, "farmers away from farms." She shakes my hand. "Criminal, husbands *working*! If *we* go"—she shakes my wrists—"*babies* will have to drive." She reaches a hand toward Floyd.

Floyd bends at the waist and brings his ankles together, politely. They shake hands.

I don't mind acknowledging Mrs. Bagnoli's energy. Her hair, which is thick and gray, a horsy sort of hair, is looped into a fountain effect on the top of her head. Small bobby pins catch the light and send out snappy flashes. She wears black tapered slacks and a black nylon blouse, over a body that is short-legged, thick-thighed, and enormously breasted. Now that she's out in the open, she looks reliable.

Floyd finishes inhaling the long breath he took in at her arrival, and lets out a low whistle. That easily, the day reassembles itself.

These are the United States, I chant in my heart. Floyd breathes with contentment, and I, for my part, am willing to take some risks. Maybe Mrs. Bagnoli was showing us she could drive.

. . .

We stand at the side of the wagon and sort out three pairs of brown cotton work gloves.

"Where's Floyd?" Mrs. Bagnoli asks me.

She means my husband, Lloyd.

"You mean *Lloyd*," I say. "My husband is Lloyd. He's with the Marry brothers," I say. "Constructing. Pole barns. *This* is Floyd. Floyd Dey."

"Floyd! All right. Whatever. It's all the same. *You* won't farm either, will you?" She points at Floyd. She wears a large black-stoned ring on her index finger.

"Nah," he says. "This is it."

"There!" she says, and snaps the gloves in her hands and turns away.

"But I like it," Floyd explains.

Mrs. Bagnoli doesn't care whether he likes it or not. She goes to the tractor and she pats her gloved hand along the fender as she walks by.

"I like it," he says again.

"So," says Mrs. Bagnoli. "Let's go." With her hands on the steering wheel, she pulls herself up onto the tractor seat.

Without hesitation, without instruction, Mrs. Bagnoli starts up the engine. Floyd and I swing onto the wagon and dangle our legs off the side. Somehow, Mrs. Bagnoli knows the trick of the brake release, and Floyd nods at me, grinning.

It doesn't take long to see that Mrs. Bagnoli is a purposeful, serious-minded woman. It's clear she commands a world-view. Small things fall away. She sits up on the blue cushion seat, her back straight, her neck like a fine stalk, very slender and pearly above the black collar of the blouse. Her hair rises and rises, then falls in sprays. She doesn't look left or right, and—as soon as the clutch is released—we *glide*, around the barn, cutting right from the lane to make a path through the weed field. We hit high weeds—Queen Anne's lace, brittle and folded flat; flowering nettle. The stalks crumple under the tractor's tires, and bristled round seeds shoot up at the sides of the wagon. The roar of the tractor disappears in the smattering of weeds.

Tractor, baler, wagon, dry weeds—all of it stirs a considerable racket, a whirring that isn't mechanical.

"Lord!" Floyd says. He stretches out on his back and pretends he's floating.

Mrs. Bagnoli drives a path that hasn't a ripple. Our teeth don't rattle; our breath doesn't catch.

In the light wind, strands of Mrs. Bagnoli's hair whip out to the side and the tips point toward us. The ground unrolls like a carpet. We drive out of the weed field into the cleared hayfield, where the alfalfa lies in windrows, one beyond another in dark, continuous breakers. The air sweeps up from the hot field and the heat, an invisible wake, spreads out behind us.

At the first windrow, Mrs. Bagnoli pulls the silvery PTO knob and the baler flywheel spins, the pickup teeth swing around to feed in hay, and the plunger takes its first dive down, pushing leaf and stalk and flower together. It's the noise of a natural catastrophe. There's a sudden heat, as if the sun capped the field and folded everything in.

Floyd and I stand up to wait for the first bale.

"Smooth!" he shouts.

We have to shout.

"Look here!" I yell. I stand with my legs apart, on tiptoe.

Floyd cocks his head to watch. I touch my toes, right fingers to left foot, left fingers to right foot. The ride is so smooth I don't have to shift for balance. I don't topple. Floyd sees the proof.

"She's the best!" he shouts. "Hang on to her!"

"She's great!"

"We're sailin, ain't we? We get that woman to drive for the government, we'd be on our way, don't you think—sailin."

"You think she's driven these fields?" I ask.

"Nah, she's a *driver*. Make her Secretary of State!"

A good many things in this world are not possible. Floyd Dey, for instance, being goodhearted, will never deeply offend. It is possible he will know happiness.

"Will you be around next summer?" I shout.

In his loudest voice, his words come slowly through the heat. "Doubt it! I want to move myself out!"

"School?"

"Western, sure! It's a great place, Kalamazoo!"

Floyd takes the first bale, a lopsided one, very loose, which he has to hug to keep it from collapsing.

"It ain't all parties!" he says for my information. "I know a guy, Arnie. He says he'll get me work!"

"What'll you study?" It's my turn, and I hook a bale.

"Haven't the faintest!" he says.

"What about Debbie?" Debbie Ames is his girlfriend, an awe-struck, intelligent girl.

Floyd doesn't hear.

"What about Debbie?"

"Debbie? Shit! I'll be on my own!"

Floyd snaps the twine on another bale; it's too loose. The bales are mushy.

"They got *fine* women in Kalamazoo, let me tell you!" he shouts. "I'll get me a fine woman! It's another place! You been there?"

Both of us jump down to tighten the handles. Mrs. Bagnoli, a driver with confidence in machinery, never looks back. Her hair sparkles, and she gazes ahead to the first steep slope, an arc of green in the blue sky ahead. Floyd and I know the requirements of the hill—we know the wagon is bolted and won't rear up—

but we pull ourselves back in a hurry and stand at the front, counterbalancing. Standing sideways, a bend to the knee, we try to give ourselves weight, although my boots slip a little with the incline. Up the slope there's practically nothing but blue.

When the tractor goes over the top and everything evens out, I shout to Floyd, "I've never been to Kalamazoo!"

"Well, it ain't like this! There's ravines! Mists!" He waves his arms to create a murkiness. "They don't build in these ravines! So you get houses, jam-packed McDonald's, and then you step out the back door and it's the *wild!* I think it does something to the women!"

"You think?"

"They *look* wild! That suits *me!* When they get out of high school, they get apartments, buy their own furniture! Plants! Arnie's got a friend, nineteen, with her own place! Everything she wants!"

Floyd is as sweet as a foreigner. He travels along, never embarrassed, not oblivious, although women are as weird to him as hors d'oeuvres. Should he use a fork or his fingers? He checks out the world-at-large, and he doesn't take disappointment. He hardly blinks. Such is the mildness of sailors in Madagascar. What a place, they say.

Bales push up from the chute, heavy and solid, emerald-green. The smell of alfalfa bloom rushes in, and a thin puff of dust rises with each bale to shoulder height and then sinks as a film on the wagon. Loading the bales, lifting a measure of heat with each one, we breathe deep breaths, and of course the hairs in Floyd's nose pick up leaves, grit.

I give him a Kleenex.

Snorting a little, coughing, he rubs at the green dust and then sticks the Kleenex into the side of his shoe.

His back shows a pattern of dampness, beads of sweat organized either side of the backbone, and a fine moisture marks his face with dark streaks, just above and below his lips.

"It's hot!" I shout.

"So sweat!"

"I am!"

Floyd pushes my shoulder to turn me around. He is looking for sweat.

"Say, your shirt's soaked! Hang the thing up!"

I consider the idea. "I'd itch! It's sticky!"

"There's an air!" he says, flapping his arms.

I look at Floyd's face and I see a downright factual face.

"It's nothing to me!" he yells.

And it's true, I see that.

"Go on!" he says.

I pull the shirt out of my jeans and yank it off.

Floyd, my buddy, takes the shirt from me and aims for an upright. He pitches, and the thing catches.

Two flags flying. All-clear.

Great huffs, like breaths from enormous lungs, remote and chill, rush against my breasts and flow around my sides. I can feel my ribs, the bend of the bones, cooling.

There's not much to do. Floyd and I have the open air in common, nothing more. We ride along, arms out, ventilating.

"Cooler, ain't it?" is what Floyd says.

The day slips out of kilter. I don't tell Floyd. Crops, the flourishing hybrids, machinery, barns—all appear isolate, diminished, doll-pretty. I feel the shrinkage. Except for my arms, elbows to wrists, my skin is as white as a tusk. There are a few pale veins across my breasts, rivery; my navel is purple with some kind of leaf.

"Mrs. Bagnoli drives steady, don't she?" Floyd says. Then he looks at me. "You just let me know if you want that shirt."

"I will," I say.

Floyd Dey will be decent in death. I see that. He will use very predictable last words. His body in death will retain its beauty, a smoothness he's rubbed with his fingertips all his life.

On the tractor, Mrs. Bagnoli's magical accord with machinery signals the load is complete. She tosses her head the way people do to discard a knot of thoughts. She twists in her seat and looks back over her left shoulder. Her eyes are large and dark, the iris and pupil matching. She sees now, behind the baler, a full wagon, four tiers high, and two human bodies in jeans, bare-chested—one easygoing, one askew, armpits open to breezes. She takes note.

"Ahoy!" she yells.

She waves an arm and shows a set of wide teeth.

The next instant, she unbuttons her black nylon blouse and slips it off.

I hear the laughing. She looks ahead, but she waves to us once again, black blouse in hand. She wears a black bra, big as the top of a swimsuit. There's wide elastic right to the hooks. Across the round of her shoulders and the flat of her upper back, Mrs. Bagnoli's skin is phenomenally white.

All of the air in the field parts around her and flows away, drastically cooled.

"She's a go-getter!" Floyd shouts.

"A go-getter?"

Floyd pulls the last bale onto the wagon, throws the chute forward, and sits himself down.

"Just look at her," Floyd says. "She's going places."

With the wagon loaded, Mrs. Bagnoli punches the PTO knob and the baler winds down. The plunger drops heavily, lifts and drops, more slowly each time. Noises sink in the ground and go off with the heat.

The three of us ride in the quiet down a long slope toward the barn. Mrs. Bagnoli swings her blouse, an automatic motion, until it winds around her arm. She swings it the other way, unwinding it. After a time, she tosses the blouse, with an aim as sure as Floyd's, onto the muffler pipe that stands in the middle of the tractor's hood. The blouse catches the stack by a sleeve, and like the ill-assorted ship that we are, masted and rigged and fitted out, we drive on, signaling God knows what.

The black blouse clings to the muffler and twists around it. In another few seconds, the fabric smokes. A white steamy smoke. Another second, and Mrs. Bagnoli's blouse is a flame, tall and yellow and nearly invisible in the sun, obscured by the terrific glare off the field, out of the sky.

But the blouse is there, and the blouse burns.

We are slow to react. When we do, we are sensible. We stand up—Mrs. Bagnoli where she is, Floyd and I on the front two bales—and we call out, in chorus: Get a stick—There ain't no stick—Get the blouse on the ground—Too dry, too dry—The gas tank!—No, don't move—Fumes—Watch out, it'll blow! Watch out!

We sit down, abruptly, the three of us, to watch the flame and register the percussion that will blind us and deafen us and stop time just where it is. Mrs. Bagnoli drives straight ahead, as if she has blissfully ceased driving.

The flame rises and falls; a weak thread of gray smoke marks the wind's direction. Then the nylon cloth separates from itself and drips in small distinguishable fires down the muffler pipe. Flames pool and drop onto the hood of the tractor and drop again into the field.

Mrs. Bagnoli doesn't shift gears or brake.

I can see, without moving my eyes, too many things—the

blouse burning, the black-and-white pattern of Mrs. Bagnoli's back; a flutter of remnant flames in the field.

It's a colorful afternoon, sweetly hushed, splashy. Disaster always feels brand-new.

But this, in the end, is the old story.

Nothing happens. The blouse burns itself out. I live to say so. We don't detonate.

When the last flames collapse, Mrs. Bagnoli stops the tractor. We're at the edge of the field and I can hear the rattle of grasshoppers and see flicks of them in the stubble. On my shoulder, I feel Floyd's breathing.

He climbs the bales and grabs our shirts. He understands civility very well—nobody runs bare-breasted to the aid of strangers.

While Floyd and I pull on our shirts and shake out our hair, Mrs. Bagnoli, up front, takes a screwdriver from the tool box and scrapes some ash off the muffler. She blows gray debris off the hood and picks up a black button or two.

"Good God! We should all be angels!" She swings herself down from the tractor.

"You okay?" Floyd calls.

"Sure," she says. "*You're* the pale one. *You* sit down."

But Floyd and I jump off the wagon and meet Mrs. Bagnoli by the side of the baler.

"Jesus," says Floyd, taking her hand. He keeps hold of Mrs. Bagnoli's hand, and he takes mine, too. The three of us do a little dance, in a circle. I catch Mrs. Bagnoli's eye.

"That was some driving!" Floyd says.

Mrs. Bagnoli frees her hands and claps a couple of times.

"I'd probably have stopped the tractor," Floyd says.

"Oh, a mistake!" Mrs. Bagnoli frowns.

Then she claps her hands again. "Let's get out of here!" In

her black bra and slacks, she climbs on the tractor and starts it up. Floyd and I jump to our places on the front bales.

"No need to tell her a thing," Floyd says.

Mrs. Bagnoli drives to the barn, parks the tractor, and we walk, side by side, Mrs. Bagnoli in the middle, to the house. Inside, I hunt up one of my white blouses for her to wear, and we sit with gin-and-tonics at the white-painted kitchen table while Floyd calls up Debbie and sets a date for later. "I got news," he says into the phone.

Mrs. Bagnoli and I get acquainted. In answer to my questions, she tells me the story of her husband's ordeal in the cement mixer. Having been so close to death, she says, he eats only steaks now for supper. I learn how many of her kids live in California, and she gets the same sort of information from me.

I will wait until another time to ask her about her future, the plans she has.

"Bye-bye, Deb," Floyd says, and joins us. He sits down and crosses his legs at the ankles. He lifts his gin-and-tonic for a toast.

"To a hell of a driver!" he says.

"Hooray!" I say.

"Hear, hear!" says Mrs. Bagnoli.

Mrs. Bagnoli and I sip at our drinks. We watch Floyd drink down his glass and head outside to start up the motor on the hay elevator. On the back step, he peels off his shirt, rolls it in a ball, and as he goes by his car, he pitches it in through the open window.

"He's steady," I say to Mrs. Bagnoli. "Very helpful."

"And such a smooth back!" she remarks.

"Yes, indeed," I agree.

"Wouldn't you say," Mrs. Bagnoli says carefully, "that he is encouraged by what he has seen of womanhood?"

"I hope so," I say. "Time will tell."

We finish our drinks and step outside. When the wagon's unloaded, it will be nearly dusk and my husband, Lloyd, will be on his way home. By dark, Floyd Dey will be deep into kisses with Debbie, and Mrs. Bagnoli will have driven to and from Bob's Market for steaks.

Already, I'm looking forward to next summer's haying. With Floyd's brother Harry T. and Mrs. Bagnoli, everything should go like clockwork. But we won't forget Floyd. I'll tell her whatever I hear from Kalamazoo. After all, Floyd and I are good friends. He'll visit at Christmas and I'll write him sometimes to keep him informed of Mrs. Bagnoli's progress toward the office of Secretary of State. Floyd is not a boy to be mystified.

Harmony

It's Saturday again. Sherry sits on the floor beside the refrigerator, her bare legs flat against the tile. She's telling me she likes sex. She's fairly general about it, but enthusiastic. "It's good when it's like swimming," she says, and she pushes her arms through the air a little. "Everything going easy, your shoulders in and out of the water, and what you're doing keeps you afloat and keeps you going. And another body, swimming along, nothing opposite about it, playing right along and rolling—Vicki, it's better than any daydreaming. You can touch everything."

Upstairs, in the kids' room, I hear something crash, not a serious noise, though, and some scrambling and stirring follows, not silence, so Sherry just stays where she is and so do I. I'm in the low-slung canvas chair beside Sherry's table of plants. Polly and Hal, Sherry's kids, pretty much take care of themselves now.

I'm not here as the baby-sitter. Since school's over, I just stop in sometimes to talk to Sherry, or she calls me up to go someplace. And Saturdays, every week, we spend together. Sherry talks about everything, and she tells me whatever she thinks. Apparently, she thinks I should hear the good side of sex. No matter what she's got hold of, Sherry acts as if she experiences some kind of special pleasures. The trouble I have is, I don't know if she's lying. Sherry might be lying. In February, she told me she liked Februarys. And it's true that I saw her one afternoon cut up a hard blue plastic back-yard sled; she scissored it into shoe-shaped footsies and super-glued them onto her sneakers, and onto the good rubber boots of her kids. With branches as poles, the three of them walked out onto the iced-over drifts to shoe-skate the neighbor's field. It didn't look easy. But she said she enjoyed it.

I'm not sure what makes real, acceptable proof. I wish I could just take her word.

Sherry says Jeff is a complex man. She says to me, when I cackle at that: "Vicki, the man is no oaf. You watch out, Vicki," she warns me, and her palms smack her knees, and her frown lines cave in, "you'll end up with one handsome bastard after another."

Then, with her kids tearing into the room and running around the kitchen table, Sherry gets up, pours me some white wine in a juice glass; she brings out the gut bucket she made with a washtub and mop handle, and while I drink and while her kids drum the chair seats, Sherry sings me her favorite song, which she made up, she says, for the sake of women everywhere in the world. "And that means you and me, too, Vicki," she adds. Like we are all poor souls, starting over at A-B-C. Anyway, she is interesting to watch, and I'm getting to like this enough to join in for the last two lines. I'm good at harmony.

I say, "Write a song for men, too, why don't you?"

"Can't be done," Sherry says.

Sherry believes she makes herself clear, with what she calls "demonstrations," which I would call good times you plan. When I baby-sat for her, she left notes saying, for instance: "Demonstration for Polly and Hal— Take dough from baggie in crisper. Sculpt a self-portrait. Don't explain. *Use your fingers.*"

I did what she said. Apparently, not explaining made it a demonstration.

Sherry has thick brown hair. Each strand is separate and crinkled. Her hair stands out from her head as if she's got herself over a sidewalk grate where a steady air is rising. What I like best about her is the gap between her front teeth, which are skewed out a little, and the two sharp frown lines between her eyebrows—because otherwise she'd be very beautiful. She has dark-green eyes, like the green you sometimes see in coal. She says she is thirty.

For the last year, Sherry's been living with Jeff, a ceramicist and a half-mute. He is a tall person, with flat cheekbones and blue eyes stretched out beneath blond eyebrows; his chin has a cleft down the middle which makes his face look like it's being torn apart from the bottom up. I pity him. He looks, I swear, like an infant smashed and stretched very suddenly into an old man.

Sherry says they stay together because things are good; sex is good. That wouldn't keep me, I don't think, even if it was the truth.

She tells me that when Jeff sleeps, he throws pots, and treadles the wheel, pumping his foot faster and faster until he runs out of breath and swings back an arm as if he's angry and is slinging the pot out the window. He's too calm in the daytime to suit me. I don't like his ideas of conversation: he refuses to talk about the weather, or food. He denies the fact that his mother still does his laundry once a week, which she does.

It's a dishonest house, is what I think.

"He pays attention," Sherry told me the day Jeff was moving in and we were cleaning out half of her closet. "He pays attention."

"To what?"

"To skin. To the body."

"What if he doesn't know anything else?"

"He knows clay."

"And what if he doesn't know anything else?"

"Vicki!" she said, stuffing brown socks, two blue Arrow shirts into a black garbage sack for Goodwill. "What the hell do you want?"

She sat down on the bed. She pulled me by the wrist and held all the fingers of my left hand in her palm. "Now shut your eyes," Sherry said. I shut my eyes. "Jeff does this." She took my fingers, one at a time, and let them slide through hers as if she were blind, or measuring, or slipping invisible rings off and on. All of her fingers felt like lips.

"There," she said. "He's no oaf."

She let go of my hand and it fell against my thigh like somebody else's hand, weighty again.

Okay, that kind of touch is something to think about. But I think there should be more to a man than good touching, so why won't Sherry tell me? Honest to God, I work at these things. I ought to learn something from Sherry, or from someone. My mother's no help, but I don't expect it from her. She is a fine, but close-mouthed, woman; she's glad enough that Sherry's the one to deal with me. My mother doesn't know it, but Sherry knows it—I've had sex, more than a couple of times. And with guys I liked. There's been interest in it, but it was nothing as smooth as swimming, and I've decided to put it off for a while and wait for some real excitement.

The best time I remember, at least the most comfortable, was at Harold's, when I rubbed him up for a while, and that was that, and he rubbed me, too, like a long-armed mechanical man, for as long as it took. The TV was going, and I watched him watching the Lansing news, from the school-board report right through the weather. We were under the influence, the weatherman said, of a low-pressure system in the Upper Peninsula.

"Never mind about the right man," Sherry tells me. "You keep your eyes open, Vicki."

I have my own thoughts about how Sherry keeps her eyes open—she blinks, looks right on through everything, and ends up watching the sky. She won't put curtains on any windows. And she tells me she's always had trouble sleeping, which I believe. She was beaten up by her father once and lost her hearing in one ear. "It brought me completely to my senses," she brags. When that happened she left home, and she's lived with several men, which she's mentioned in connection with ashtrays or stitches or stealing. She had Polly and Hal; she was married twice. Oafs, I suppose—lousy touchers.

So far, with the baby-sitting, I've picked up this kind of thing: recipes for rice dishes, plenty of kids' games, a little about anthropology, which is the subject Sherry studies at MSU. These aren't items that Sherry thinks of as learning, however. I agree with her there. I'm interested in learning, for instance, if she knows what she's talking about when she says she enjoys sex. When she says she enjoys life.

Sherry will have her degree at the end of the summer and she wants to move to Chicago in the fall. If she leaves, Jeff plans to "digress," as he calls it; he'll try out Detroit, "the hotbed of potting," he says, looking serious and sad, with a hand on each side of his chin, his eyes straight on Sherry.

Given the uncertain future, Sherry and I have been spending Saturdays this summer together, hunting up "Beautiful Views of

Jackson." It's a real project. Sherry puts a red-headed pin in the map taped to her kitchen wall whenever we come back with a place we can both agree is a beautiful view. She complains about how mapmakers always make the wrong kind of maps, showing only obvious features. The Fourth of July, we were checking a map for the way out to Napoleon to see the fireworks. "Who wants a map of animal trails?" Sherry pointed to the intersection of First and Morrell. "They could put in grazing patches, rocks. Shelters. We'll make a *meaningful* map, Vicki," she said, and that's how these Saturdays started.

I wouldn't have believed you could put together a meaningful map of Jackson, but it hasn't been going too badly. So far, we've stuck in six pins. In the last survey *Life & Living* took of Michigan cities, Jackson came in last, as the worst place to live, and Sherry said, "Naturally. Nobody sees the beautiful views." I agree with that. What they point out downtown are a couple of banks and a couple of steel buildings and two blocks of potholed mall. The Penney's store has three floors but, even so, what they do is stack jeans on two tables in the basement, by the wall display of pillows and bedpads, honest to God. There's one piece of sculpture in front of the Sheraton, but the men come in from an underground parking lot, up the elevator, to register, and nobody sees the front entrance except for the walk-ins. How many walk-ins do you get at the Sheraton?

We decided against marking objects and points of interest on our map: the sculpture is big and listed in the books; the four-trunked elm of Fourth Street is a commonplace; and Little Mary's Grave with the carved, sexed cupids is public, junior-high knowledge. I went there like everyone else in eighth grade, a moonless night, to touch the cupid. You touch the granite cupid of the opposite sex until you shiver, which isn't long for anybody, and Sherry says the chill is still half of Jackson's idea of orgasm.

She said skip it.

She wants larger views. She wants each pin to mark a place you can sit and sit for a long time and not get tired looking. She gave me instructions about finding angles where the light is especially good, where buildings come together in interesting ways, where colors of plants and smells and everything combine to make some whole thing worth looking at. The first red pinhead on Sherry's map was the view from a slab in the vacant lot opposite Francis and Cortland, where a bricked-up six-story building marks the end of the mall. Four stories up, a mission church from around the corner has painted its name in huge blue cursive letters. You sit on the slab and you see the bricks and the blue letters, and the morning sun's on your back.

Last Saturday, at the edge of a swamp by the railroad yards, Sherry said, "In the fall, Vicki, you'll want to have places like this. Show your boyfriends. It'll be a good test."

"For what?"

"For your boyfriends!"

"You bringing *Jeff* around to these views?" I asked.

"Vicki, you're sly," Sherry said. "You're a sly one."

She picked a cattail right where she was, bent the stalk, and sailed it off. "Sometimes they fly back," she told me. She held both hands at her eyes for shade. "Like a boomerang," she said.

That I don't believe. At all.

From where we were in the swamp, we could see the back end of the railroad yards, the hulk of the old roundhouse, and a good bit of debris from the place—bent rails, a box of rusty spikes, miscellaneous metal—heaped at the edge of the water.

Farther behind us, across a stretch of reddish, slimed water, was one of the largest muskrat houses I'd ever seen, a structure of sticks maybe six feet wide and about as high. On top, two turtles soaked in the sun, shining like coins.

"From where they are," Sherry said, "it would be a view. What do you think?"

"I suppose," I said, balking. Which I am good at, having learned that much in school.

I tramped around, looking for other ways to get the whole panorama of two dozen tracks, the gutted roundhouse, with plenty of swamp in the foreground. But I had to agree she was right. Over the water, the view would be better.

Sherry took off her shoes and started in.

Just about then, some clown from the railroad yards, far away, blew a goddamn whistle and started toward us.

"Hey! Hey, you, there!" he was yelling, or yelling something. He jumped on a stack of crossties and I could see a bright red cap, a beard, a red shirt, and light pants. Then he was coming at us again.

Sherry called to me, "Get over here. Move it."

She was already somehow across the water. Her light-blue jeans were a mess from the slime, which must have gone nearly up to her waist, and there she sat, dripping, on the muskrat's heap of branches and sticks, shaking her hands and arms, drops flying all around.

One thing with Sherry, you don't get much choice. I didn't even pull off my shoes for fear of underwater metal. I didn't breathe; I didn't want smells to deal with, too. I just strode in, with my lips tight together, and sloshed along. It wasn't pleasant. But it also wasn't too far across. Sherry gave me her hand and I was perched up on top of the muskrat house beside her with room to spare.

The view was a good one. The railroad man, a slash of red in the cattails, was a nice touch.

He could see we were just sitting there doing nothing, but he came along anyway. Pretty soon, he stood like a cop at the edge of the water, a silver whistle around his neck; he puffed himself up and when he breathed, his lips rolled up, pink, like something alive moved in his beard.

"You looking for something?"

"No," we both said.

"You ladies hunting a man, that it?"

I stuck out my tongue.

"Sure!" said Sherry. "Come on over."

"Watch it now, girlies. I'll get the whole crew out here and that'll be something to see." He had his hands on his hips, like a coach.

"You go, we go!" Sherry called back. "Come on over. One man is plenty."

Honest to God. I just looked at her. You liar, you crummy liar, I thought.

"Trespassers, ladies, don't give out orders," the man said. He smiled, open-mouthed, through the beard. "*I'm* the one says do we use cuffs or not."

With one hand, he reached around into the back pocket of his pants.

"What'll it be?" he said. "You slip on across, or I handle this some other way?"

It was hot in that stinking swamp, hot as a foreign country. My jeans were steaming. The man kept smiling his open-wide smile and didn't once take his eyes off Sherry.

Sherry pulled herself up a little and hunkered there, like she wanted her good ear closer to him, for quiet conversation. But she kept the baby talk going.

"Come *here*. There's a great view."

Well, he laughed at that, the black hole of his mouth sending up noise, and he swung an arm around. The hand was missing the thumb. I could see the stump, pearly, glistening.

"You're the view, lady," he said to Sherry. "I got you right in my eye. Say I cuff your feet, how far you think you'll get?" His voice dropped. "You nod to trouble, you got it."

Sherry stood up, and there were small sticks and brown streaks of mud on her shirt sleeves. I thought she was going to go help him in. But she pointed: "What happened there to your thumb?"

The man leaned far over, as if for some reason he had to bend down to see his thumb. The toes of his boots pressed into the wet. When he stood up, his lips went shut in a pink line.

"Lady," he said, "you want this simple or not?" The man was across twenty feet of water, alone and clean and thumbless, and you could tell he was less and less happy about it.

"I want you over here," Sherry said, serious as when she called her kids. "I'll comb your hair, honey—look." Sherry combed her hair upward with her fingers. Some of it stayed standing up. She bent over me, and she demonstrated again, with my hair, what her combing could do. Her fingers pulled through my hair and I could feel hot air reach right to my skull bone. Sherry recited him a list of what she would do, and it was quite an accounting. "Vicki won't mind, will you, Vicki?"

"Ha."

"Sure. Vicki's no kid."

Sherry'd say anything once she saw that she was in charge. She isn't subtle. But she knows how far a person will finally go, and which direction. She sets things up, Sherry does.

"You lose your thumb in the yards?" Sherry asked the man. "In Korea?" She'd guessed his age, I bet; anyway, I had.

The man just stood there, looking at her. I heard a red-wing blackbird trilling nearby.

"Korea," the man said, calm. "And the tip of the little finger."

He held his hand up; he pulled the shirt sleeve back, and I could see it was true.

Sherry sat down, cross-legged, on the muskrat house. "I have all my fingers," she said.

The poor man was standing, just standing, at the edge of the water in his red shirt.

"You live around here?" he asked.

"No," Sherry lied. I'd call it a lie.

"Too bad," he said. "I'd walk you home." And that's when he turned and went back the way he'd come.

That swamp closed in. The sun was straight overhead and the water was flat, burning. The muskrat house, it turned out, was not built for human weight, and the mess had sunk quite a way into the water, spreading sticks out on all the sides, the middle squashing.

Sherry lay back like a woman on a beach, even so. She pushed her hair back from her face and shut her eyes. I could see that the sun was hurting her eyes through the lids; she was squinting, and her face was filled with lines, and I could see her setting her eyes up under the eyelids, up and slightly back. She breathed as if she were comfortable. As usual. Behind me, I heard the red-wing again, its throaty gargle, closer than before. Sherry sat up and turned herself around, to look out that way, too, where there was nothing to see but flat greenish swampland to the horizon. We could have been looking out over China; we could have been in the rice fields trying to figure something out.

"This a view this way, Vicki?" she asked me.

"No."

"Well," she asked next, kind of harrumphing, "was he an oaf?"

"Jesus! What do you mean? He was almost as bad as you!"

"Vicki, look," she said, quiet, but straightening up, and folding her hands the way a kid folds them up to pray at the table. "Think about his hands. Vicki, I'm serious—a man who's lost a thumb is worth some attention. To start with. Vicki, I swear."

"What if he'd stomped right on over?"

"He'd have walked us home."

"Ha!"

"It's the truth," she said. And that's all she said.

We worked our way out of the swamp, across the west end of the yards, and out onto the sidewalk of Page Avenue, me making squishing footprints and splattering drops that went dark for a second on the pavement before the heat took them, and Sherry making sucking noises with her cheeks. When we got to her place, we stuck a pin in the map, and Sherry poured some wine and handed it over as if it capped an afternoon when she'd proved something to me. Something simple: life is sweet; life is incorruptible. She thinks she's living proof.

I swear she has figured out how to ignore nine-tenths of all she knows. Honest to God, she can stretch a view. I think it's a pity. She doesn't expect enough. She'd love a body for thumblessness, Jackson for a swamp, and probably the rest of life for that.

She wears me out. Today I just want to take it easy. I don't want to have to make up my mind, or say true or false.

Sherry is twirling with Polly around the kitchen, faking a sour face; she sees I'm not much for moving out of the chair. We haven't decided yet where we're going. Sherry's idea is to head toward the bus station and take the back alley to Paka Plaza; she thinks that whole area has possibilities. By the end of summer, she wants a good map, and I tell her we'll have it.

We will.

But today I hope we stay put.

Sherry says I am easy to read, so she'll probably say next, "Vicki, let's just sit around." I don't even care if she calls it some kind of event—which she will. All I want to do is take her gut bucket out on the back step and strum a couple of old tunes.

At Odds

When Asunción Smith moved into my father's house, I was too young to catch the ridiculous sound of her pet name for me, which was Bobby-Boo. She was small, with a small voice like a recording. I was ten. For a year we were just the same height, and I had a fine time learning her fancy ways of folding paper napkins. The two of us, without cutting, made pointed paper crowns to set on our plates at the start of supper, or paper tulips, or twin-sailed boats.

My father brought Asunción in from Akron. I can't explain it. My father was a thoughtless man. I never saw him act stupid or mean, but I think it is fair to say that he never gave a thought to anything. This is not to claim he had no ideas. He had ideas. But they just blew up inside his head, with nothing clear-cut about them, and no connections to anything either. He didn't believe in motives, for instance. People did what they did. If he brought Asunción in from Akron, it was because he brought Asunción in from Akron.

Her first night at the house, Asunción tucked me in. She turned out the light by the door—and in the dark of the room, she felt her way to my bed and sat on the edge, rocking. I think her feet didn't reach the floor. She whispered, "I am happy, Bobby-Boo. I am full of joy that you are here because, you see, I will miss my mother."

"I miss my sister," I said.

"Oh, but she is not far away," Asunción said. "Distance, Bobby-Boo, that is the thing. Your sister is close at hand." Then she kissed me on the head, told me to shut my eyes.

I preferred Asunción's style of good-night to my father's. He'd developed the practice of closing the day with summary. He pulled a chair near my bed, and sat there the way he sat in a lawn chair, upright, his legs pushed out straight in front of him. He didn't lounge. And he left the ceiling light on, setting our discussion in the tell-all light of a discount store. My father would ask me to recite my adventures of the day, and he'd tell me about his at work, exactly, and in sequence. Last, we went over the highlights of the national news. When that was finished, my father patted both my knees and kissed both my cheeks. His pale face, twice as wide as mine, bent close, and with each kiss I looked into one of his eyes—the left brown one, the right blue one. "Mixed heritage," was his account of this phenomenon. "I got one eye from each parent," he said. "So did you."

I have two blue eyes. With both of them, I'd watch my father walk to the door, flick off the light switch, and take two steps into the hall. It was from there that he said good-night.

For that instant, in the doorway, he appeared faceless and colorless, a cut-out cardboard shape, not one feature. The dim configuration, or a memory of it, held for another second. But he could have been anyone. At bedtime, without thinking how it looked, my father said good-night in the dark.

Although I believe my father was smart, even clever, he did nothing to promote that impression. Probably the worst thing he did, from my point of view, was cut his hair, by setting the mixing bowl on his head and clipping around it, the way doltish characters do in the cartoons, His hair was coarse and blond, with enough of a curl, thank heavens, to recoil from the severity of this style. But he didn't *look* bright with a round head of hair, and he must have known it. I was surprised to see how often Asunción pushed her fingers through his hair, captured twists of it in her fists, and kissed the tips.

With Asunción's arrival, I found it more and more a puzzle to determine what was ridiculous and what was not. The problem persists. I don't blame Asunción Smith; I don't blame my father. Nothing looked silly to them. A person could have a vicious streak, a person could be a twit, but they refused to rule it as out of the ordinary. To them, there was just people, and that was all they were going to say about it.

Life was livable. Days, my father worked at a small auto-parts plant in town, operating a screw machine. He'd done it for fourteen years. In his nightly listings, I heard numbers and types of parts produced, the daily adjustments, the retooling. When I was very small, he brought home little parts in plastic bags for me to play with—one-inch hollowed tubes, aluminum latches, brass caps.

My father was also something of a mechanic, and on weekends and evenings, he worked in the old barn out back, overhauling tractor engines, or welding. Things broke. He seemed to know how. Some things could be put back together. Some couldn't. The barn looked broken to me—it was gray, unheated, doorless, with machinery and parts half in, half out—and the whole affair leaned severely toward the ditch behind it. But my father told me the barn would not fall over.

"How do you know it won't blow over?"

"It won't."

"But how do you *know?*"

"There are physical laws," he said.

When the neighbor girl, in an illness, saw an angel by her bed smiling and blowing kisses, my father took me into the hallway, held my hand in both his hands, and in a voice that rejoiced, said, "The *brain*, Bobby-Boo. The brain is a wonder."

Even my unrest, my mulling now, would make sense to my father. He'd say, "That's Bobby-Boo, he never quits."

Against his intentions—probably because he had none—my father, and Asunción, too, contributed to my early sense of life as mystery—unaccountable, inexplicable. If thought was real, my father knew there were synapses to account for it. If love was real, my father knew there were hormones and physical variables to generate it. In this way, he appreciated the power of the moon. "Look at that light, Bobby-Boo," he'd say to me at full moon, as the three of us sat on the hood of the car in the driveway, or lay on our backs there and stared. "Nothing romantic about it!"

Because he was sensible, my father lived in awe. He laughed at psychology; he laughed at witchcraft. "We're here because we're here," he sang in a thin tenor voice when I blew out the candles on the cake at every birthday supper.

Minute by minute, anything could happen. There was no tomorrow, no idiot dreaming. I grew up expecting anything.

It was precisely a year, to the day, from the day my mother left home that Asunción Smith moved in. I don't think my father noticed the coincidence. It wouldn't have interested him. My mother, the year before, left us to live with Earl Bouse in an apartment overlooking Main Street in Osseo. Earl was a red-headed young plumber who had worked off and on for two days at a leak in our well house. He finally fixed it. He wiped his muddy hands on his shirt and waved good-bye to my mother. My mother appreciated his efforts, and said so in a candid "Note of Thanks" in the *Post-Gazette:*

To our plumber and friend
whose valuable time
gives us health and well-being,
my deepest appreciation—
Vanetta Robley.
This is to Earl Bouse.

My mother took my sister, Laurel, with her and, out of a sense of fairness, I suppose, left me with my father.

He did not appear to suffer.

Sundays he took trips to visit friends in Akron. He came back talking about all the interesting women he'd met. He mentioned Asunción Smith more than once, how she was short, how her voice twanged like a banjo. If he suffered somewhere inside, it was near the core, and it didn't show. His face, the day of my mother's desertion and every day thereafter, retained the clean and guilt-free pallor of a man who's never known rage. He said he would rather not talk about my mother, but he said it kindly. My father seemed not to have, in a personal sense, the typical masculine reflexes of hate or jealousy or fear—he was no bully— nor did he invite opinions of tragedy, or evil. My father was un-tainted. Lately, when I look at his two-toned eyes, I realize that my father is not a man of his times, not a man of his community.

But in those days, a boy myself, I sat at my bedroom window, bitterly sad at the loss of my sister, vaguely sad at the absence of my mother, believing that it was my condition of childhood alone that poured the suffering on me instead of on him. I expected, given the evidence of my father, that one day, I, too, would grow up, and I would be as full and whole and thoughtless as he.

Still, he looked like a fool. A generous spirit can do that to a man. And I saw that if my father didn't grieve for his own sake, he could grieve for the sake of others. When he read about accidents in the paper, tears filled his eyes, nearly to the edges. He made himself study the obituaries, and the younger the departed, the more surviving children, the more my father declared, "Oh, this rips at the heart." A few times, on bright Sunday mornings, he took me to the graves of neighbors, or of strangers he'd read about. We'd pick some wild daisies and set them where he guessed the heart should be. But for himself, my father was frugal with feeling. He would not have wanted me to look at him and think, oh, very sad.

Asunción carried her clothes from Akron in a brown paper sack. Everything fit into one dresser drawer. The only other possession she brought to our house was a burlap bag of seed potatoes.

My father and I helped her carry the bag into the cellar, where she arranged some boards as slats, and we placed the sack in the darkest corner. Once a week, through the winter, she went down the cellar steps to check on the potatoes. I'd go along. She'd open the tie at the top and say, "Sniff, Bobby-Boo. Sniff." We sniffed in and out of the bag. If there was a stink, we'd start unpacking potatoes, setting them carefully on newspapers on the floor, feeling each one over until we found a soft, blackening one. Asunción would wrap it in paper and hand it to me—"Now pitch *that* in the weeds."

One Saturday in March, Asunción woke me up. She sat on

the edge of my bed and whispered in her wiry voice, close to my ear, "I'm going for paint. Will you get the tires?"

"Tires?"

"Sure, we need tires. Out of the ditch, you roll out a dozen tires. Okay? Just into the yard."

I said okay. I had a picture of what she wanted.

Her first day with us, Asunción had shown me an old Polaroid of her mother visiting in Akron. In the photo, on the steps of a school bus, were two blurred women; her mother was the fuzzier one, with her hands pulled up over both sides of her face, nearly covering her eyes. The bus was parked in a yard strewn with orange-painted tires, a garden arrangement of old tires, tall plants, and small blooming flowers growing up out of them.

When Asunción showed me the picture, I wasn't afraid to ask, "You lived in a school bus?"

"Oh, sure."

"Did it work?"

"Did it *work*?"

"Did it run, as a bus?"

"Oh, no," she said. "Not at all."

She'd propped the Polaroid picture on the windowsill over the sink. So I saw the bus and the tires whenever I washed my hands, or scraped carrots, or dried the dishes. And once, once when I was drying dishes, Asunción Smith told me about her mother and the tires, how she'd grown potatoes with no rain. "She's in trouble now," Asunción said, "but then, when I was a girl, we had the world in our pocket, you know. She pulled water up, using stones, using tires. Water comes to stones and rubber. It was her discovery. She got stones. Then in these stony places, between them, she planted the eyes of her potatoes and covered them up with more stones, and then she put tires around them. She worked potatoes so much that she began to see, this is true, through their eyes. She could see with the eyes of potatoes. She could see the water coming up from the ground and she could see the feet overhead if something walked in the garden. She says whatever you take to yourself is an extra power, and her power was she could see with the eyes of potatoes. But it was the start of her sadness. She was seeing a dog one night in the garden. She saw it stepping between the rocks overhead, and digging, and she went there, and shot, and she shot the dog in the garden. Next, I don't like to say it, she saw a thief, with the eyes of the potatoes she knew there was a thief. She took her gun and she shot the thief. That was her trouble, and she couldn't stay. In Akron, nobody knows. She is careful."

"Does Father know about her?" I asked.

"Oh sure. It is a terrible story, but there it is," Asunción said.

She took the car to get paint, and I was alone in the house. My father was working that morning, overtime, one of the rare Saturdays when he was gone. I lay in bed until I heard the car turn from the drive onto the road toward town. Then I pushed my feet out, down to the bare floorboards, and sat up. More clearly than usual, I saw my room—the alarm clock lying on its face on the chest; some volumes of the *World Book*, the bindings in strings, on the floor by my bed. When I stood up, I felt how my shoulders opened out to make room for my bones. I smelled my skin. I put my nose into the crook of my elbow and breathed.

On my way to the kitchen, I walked on an orange runner in the hallway, a bristly thing Asunción had bought to brighten up the house. My mother's way of dealing with ugliness had been to cut it back to essentials. She took out rugs and peeled off wallpaper. If a board was loose on the porch, my mother ripped it out. By the time she left home, the porch was a scaffolding, and the rooms inside looked as if people had moved out years ago. But Asunción decorated.

It wasn't until I got milk out of the refrigerator that I registered a pull across my stomach: it was orange paint she was after! The idea shook me. I couldn't have said why. Even a child has a sense of rightness in some matters, and I knew that orange tires would not be right, not here.

But I drank my milk, and between sips I pushed a slice of bread in the toaster. I sat at the table. My legs felt long, and I stretched them out. I stretched out my arms. It was quiet. The air smelled of lemon and suds, very soothing. My father, who washed the dishes before he left for work, squirted Joy into the dishrag every time he rubbed a dish. Sometimes tiny bubbles floated through the kitchen long after he'd gone.

I ate the toast and headed out to the ditch—down three steps of the back porch, down the concrete walk to the driveway, and across the drive to the barn. Behind the barn, in the direction the barn was leaning, was our dump—a ditch half filled with oil drums, rusted fencing, tires, household junk. I walked to the edge of the ditch, aware I was breathing. In the dump, the huge overgrowth of raspberry and wild grape was still brown and fallen from winter, but everything lay in pleasant, natural heaps of rust and earth-colored trash.

What Asunción asked for wasn't easy—rolling some tires up out of the ditch and into the yard. We called it a ditch, but it was a ravine, maybe something trenched in the past for drainage, although there was no water in it.

I slid down the side of the ditch, digging in my heels, and the dirt that scraped away smelled like woods dirt, matted on top with leaves, with a spongy soil underneath, full of early roots, a web of white threads. At the bottom, I leaned against the ditch wall and did some figuring. One section of the slope, with some climbing zigzag bends, would work for rolling the tires up and out of the ravine. From the sprawl of tires, I marked a dozen in my mind. I tried to find some matching brands, but I had to settle for twelve of similar size and tread.

Two circles, four inside, eight out, with enough space between to walk, that's how Asunción said she wanted them arranged when she got back. She opened the trunk of the car, and I read *Tangerine* on the lids of paint cans. I helped unload the cans from the car. I helped her with the painting, too. We kneeled on the ground and brushed and brushed—it sounded like scrubbing.

"Sniff," Asunción said. She tapped the grass between the tires. So I sniffed. The ground around my elbows smelled wormy and cold.

"It's spring," I said.

"Exactly right," Asunción said. Then we went back to painting, and when we'd finished up, we hauled rocky dirt from the field beyond the barn, me shoveling and Asunción pushing the wheelbarrow, one load for each tire.

We took a lunch break and then, together, we hauled the bag of seed potatoes up from the cellar. "Now, I must show you this about planting the eyes," Asunción said. She gave me a paring knife and demonstrated how to slice the potato and cut out the eyes; each potato multiplied into many, and we planted these pieces inside the rims of the tires. Asunción said, "When the plants die away, we lift the tires, we roll them around, and out fall big potatoes, perfect. I tell you this from experience."

The tires, precise orange circles—a circle within a circle—lay on the lawn, smoothed mounds of brown dirt in their centers. They looked like foreign objects, something displaced, radioactive, rampant.

Asunción and I stood there and sighed. It had taken all day,

and it was something to see, all right—an armada from outer
space.

That Saturday, as on a regular workday, my father's ride dropped
him off at the end of the driveway. He walked toward the back
door, scraping the toes of his shoes, making two narrow trails in
the gravel. He hadn't cut his hair since early winter, and some
blond curls swung fore and aft of his ears.

I was folding the burlap bag, on my knees near the porch.
Asunción stood to the side of the tires, both arms raised into the
dusk, posing in a grand gesture of presentation.

When my father saw the tableau, he stopped. He set his lunch-
box down on the driveway—he just dipped his knees and set it
down flat. Then he put his arms out in front of him, and opened
them up slowly, one of those huge, foolhardy embraces that takes
in everything.

"Wouldn't you know!" he said. "Wouldn't you know!"

"Bobby-Boo helped," Asunción said.

"*Did* he?" my father said. He put his whole hand to his face
and he threw me a kiss. "Good for you, Bobby-Boo!"

I felt ridiculous.

I felt very proud.

I'd say that was the first day I felt like myself. All wrong. At
odds. It doesn't matter what I do.

Breaking the News
to Doll

Doll is one of the Fethers, who are known for contentment. They marry second cousins their own age and populate the northern reaches of Jerome Road with unblinking, blond children. In Jerome, on any road, it's acceptable to say, Hi, Fether, to every child. Years ago, Doll married her cousin Daniel, and this past year, with all of her children but D.J. married, she brought back her father, the loudest Fether, to live in the farmhouse. She thought she should, and she wanted to. Doll, predictably, quiets him when the talk about farming builds up feeling and veers to extremes.

Father Fether pushes his fingertips toward his heart; he thumps his chest like a melon. "They want Russians to starve, and they're starving *us*. Am I a gambler? Have I ever lost money on this farm before? I am asking you." Doll smiles and rests her arms, open-

palmed, on the table. "Daddy," she says, softly. "Oh, Daddy."
That's all it takes.

Doll guards the world's crust as one would blown glass; her
instincts require keeping boys and men light-footed and shushed,
so the world does not crack. Doll's silence is always kindly, un-
spiteful, and she is admired in Jerome for raising three boys whom
the law has never touched. They did as they should. They drank
beer in the barn. What they knew about drugs or sex nobody
could say. These boys passed English in high school, and the
two youngest married their girlfriends, distant Fethers, without
display. D.J., the oldest, somewhat slower, and more of a smiler
than his mother, stayed on in the north bedroom of the upstairs,
and helped out his father on the farm.

Once a week, on Wednesdays, Doll visits Amanda von Schmittou in her apartment over Penny's Plumbing, on Main Street in
Jerome. Doll wants to visit her, and not completely out of pity.
They sit at the kitchen table, Amanda full of gestures and outrage,
and Doll becalmed, wide-eyed, sometimes listening to the Hills-
dale station on the radio on top of the refrigerator.

Amanda, with black hair and a cockeyed nose, is no Fether;
Doll accepts that. She's used to it. Over the years, Doll has spent
time with Amanda, through her long marriage to Gaylord von
Schmittou, when Amanda established herself on a farm at the
edge of town, and then the brief time with Richmond, Gaylord's
father, who brought Amanda around to her latest theme: the
celebration of aged men. On this subject, as on others, Doll
expects to be exhausted by Amanda's talk. When she leaves the
apartment, Doll holds the cold handrail going downstairs, and
in her car, Doll leans her head back on the seat and shuts her
eyes a few moments before turning the key and starting home.

Amanda is like a sister—Doll once told her father—who likes
to talk. And since Amanda isn't a Fether, Doll allows her, in
the subtle ways Doll can allow, a range of expression, a severity

of tone, that no one in the Fether family would ever be granted
for long. Doll shifts her eyes up to the radio sometimes, and lets
Amanda rant and get up and down in her speeches. Doll knows
her own graciousness. Her husband, Daniel, praises her, and
touches her shoulders gently, and calls her his cloud when he
wakes her up in the middle of the night.

"I don't tell you anything about old men but the truth," Amanda
says, still at the doorway, in the cold air from the hall.

Doll thinks, her chin lifted.

"Old men," Amanda says, "cough with a kind of ignorance.
They think they're alone in the room." Amanda kicks the door
shut. She takes Doll by one hand and leads her to the kitchen
table. "You marry an old man, your life tips over. It's reckless.
You'd better sit down, Doll, and take this in. I'm talking about
the lively ones, Doll. They have skin like satin around the navel.
And nerve. They got nothing to lose."

Doll, who is wide-faced, with rich cream-colored skin and
apricot dreamy eyes, sits in a Samsonite folding chair at Amanda's
table and gives herself over to listening. It's March, and the chilled
air from her walk down the sidewalk in town still surrounds her.
She rubs a ruby ring and looks straight across to Amanda. As a
favor, she can make herself into a better audience than the PTA
crowd, more devoted, more hushed. Her face accumulates all
the signs of full comprehension. She brightens with talk, and
eventually she nods. She sits very straight, smiles with red lips
drawn in a wide curve, and twists with her thumb and forefinger
one of the red curls by her right ear.

"It wasn't Gaylord that got me thinking, that much will make
some sense to you," Amanda says. She throws an arm back toward
an overstuffed chair in the corner. The arm falls on the table,
awkwardly. It's a pale arm, splotched with large freckles.

Doll nods and reaches over to squeeze Amanda's wrist. She pities Amanda for her losses: Gaylord, dead on his own; and then recently, Richmond, killed by a tree. Doll's touch is the wordless salve of a healthy woman with three men at home: her Daniel in the bedroom downstairs and, upstairs, her daddy and a grown blond boy.

"Gaylord's death," Amanda confides, pressing Doll's wide fingertips, "was a slow, visible dissolve. He told me one morning he was a sick man. 'I'm a sick man,' he said. Just that, after his eggs. Without any change in the color in his face. He was always right. He zipped up his windbreaker and drove himself to the doctor, who predicted he'd pale—'You will surely pale'—the doctor told him that much, which he did, while those large time-release capsules, the really large ones, broke apart and washed away through his bloodstream. There are surging sounds in the plumbing of the laundromat, Doll, and the mild smells there, too, that remind me of those days."

Doll smiles. She smiles without shifting her shoulders or moving her head.

"But Gaylord took good advice—he believed everybody," Amanda says, her voice pitching upward, "and he died on schedule. *He* knew he was dying on schedule. 'So! What is the virtue of regularity?' I asked him. Resolute as he was, and you know he was, he had certainly been disheartened with me for many years, I know that, although not at the end, Doll, when I drove him around to see the leaves in the Irish Hills. 'This is a pretty spot,' he said to me, and he meant it, one turn after another. 'This is a pretty spot.' " Amanda rubs her arms, up and down, warming them. Doll knows this part, how Gaylord sank back into the bucket seat, with his head cocked away toward the window, how he put his hands like empty, fake hands on his knees, and how, with the skin pulled against the finger bones, he looked, as Amanda liked to say, like a pope in his chair. "He smiled and smiled that last day. But that isn't the point, Doll. The point is his papa. *You* know what I think. Richmond was prettier, so much prettier. It was another life, with him. 'The older the better,' he said, and he was persuasive, right from the start. 'You take on somebody past eighty, past it all,' was his first advice."

"You took it," Doll says.

"Younger ones try to do everything right. Gaylord took too much care. He did everything right."

"Yes, he did," Doll says, with slow lips.

"For what good reason? Lord, what I want now, what I'm going after, is somebody careless, old enough to be careless. I know what I'm saying, Doll." Amanda puts her elbows on the table. "Name me a very old man, Doll."

Doll considers. She's counting, farm to farm.

"To tell you the truth," Amanda says, "I can't see how else to live, without that kind of trouble around the house. Look at me, not gray." She pushes all her black hair toward the top of her head. "Look at this arm, Doll. Fine muscles, feel this. I'd be happy with an old man. Later, you understand, I could be happy by myself."

"You are happy now," Doll observes.

"Well, I'm not mourning," Amanda says, upright, and going to the sink. She brings Doll a glass of water. "I'm coming right back for more."

"More?" Doll asks. She glances at the wide gray radio, where Professor Garcia is closing out his half-hour show, summarizing various herbal cures of Amazonian tribes. Doll hears water boiling in Amanda's stainless-steel kettle.

"More trouble, and one more old man," Amanda says. She swings around from the stove. On her way to the table, her cup of instant tea steams and rattles; drops spill to the floor. "With a very old man, it's a relief—not knowing what to expect. And I don't mean worry about the cash, Doll. Forget Social Security.

Forget the points that Crop-Aid docks for weeds. When an old man walks out the door, the world's nice and unpredictable. Nobody's safe." Amanda sits for a moment; then she's on her feet again.

"Tea makes you jumpy," Doll says, rubbing the ruby ring.

"Oh, it's good enough tea. But I worry about how they make it into little balls," Amanda says. She goes to the counter for the tea jar and spreads a few of the instant grains on the table.

Doll presses her thumb on them and rolls them between her fingers. She tastes four or five of the tiny balls.

"Good," Doll says, and nods.

"When Richmond took out the chainsaw that day—I didn't warn him," Amanda says. "I never warned him. He knew what he was doing. You remember, Doll. You don't say to an old man, 'Sit in this chair. Die here.' "

"He had very large ears," Doll says.

"Oh, yes! You remember that! They had white hair, like down, on them, didn't they? They were velvet ears. They fit in the palms of my hands."

Amanda drinks her tea. Doll sips the water.

"He knew what was coming, Doll. The tree snapped the wrong way, and it fell. And kept falling. I think he put his arms out, like a lover, Doll."

In a moment, Doll knows, Amanda will smile, her lips pulled in against her teeth, and her teeth pressed together.

It doesn't matter to Doll that Amanda has ideas. But it's a disturbance, sitting in the apartment, after years of visits to the farm, and Doll does sit more stiffly here, where there are filmed, pressed-glass windows, and where the radio seems like a window. With the loss of the farm, and the leaning front porch, Amanda lost some respectability. Doll liked the von Schmittou farm: it was a believable place in the open. The fields began out back, beyond a ravine, and they sloped away toward a wood, unevenly. In those days, Doll and Amanda walked to the woods and back while water for tea heated on Amanda's three-burner gas stove. Doll had a chance to point out nests and pull off the tops of weeds when they walked.

Doll looks at the radio and hears the orchestra working behind Darley Management's thin voice. He holds a note. More violins come in for the end.

"Doll, do you understand? Look here." Amanda reaches over and pats Doll's right hand. "What I'm saying is, Doll—I think I'll go for your daddy."

"Daddy?"

"Doll, look at his forehead. It's beautiful, Doll. Believe me, I want to hold his head in my arms." Amanda is gesturing, hugging air.

Doll touches her lips to the water glass and waits for the end of the song. The disc jockey gives the year of the song. "Oh, Amanda," Doll says.

Amanda goes back to the stove for more hot water. She is awkward. Her arms and legs move variously, randomly; she wears toneless, unnoticeable clothes, today a black sweater, black cotton slacks, no shoes. On the linoleum floor, her feet must be cold. There was a snow on the weekend. When she leans with an elbow on the counter, waiting for the water to boil again, Doll notices her slouch and remembers that her walk outside is also a crumpled walk. She should ask Amanda her age.

Amanda says nothing. She leans back, twisted, and looks at Doll. The radio gives the hourly news update, stories disappearing like heat up to the ceiling.

"Are you keeping warm?" Doll asks. She shifts slightly in her chair.

"Of course." Amanda straightens up at the counter. She pours more hot water into her cup and sits down at the table. "And I went for a walk yesterday, out to the lake. The snow's melted some places. There was pepper-and-salt opening up down in the dirt. Remember that south hill where the sun gets through?" She stops and stares at Doll. "We should walk next week."

"Daddy says next winter he's going to Florida," Doll says, firmly.

"A Fether in Florida! Ridiculous. He told me he's going to sit in his room and swear next winter."

"He did?"

"He will, Doll."

"He does swear."

"Well, the man is unpleasant, Doll, and that's a good thing. His eyes are sinking into his skull, have you seen that? The other day, I looked in at him at the barber's, and he looked very good through the glare of the plate glass. For a while I thought the glass magnified his head, but I stepped in there to say hello, and he looked the same inside, his skin shining, and polished. When he laughs, he looks very pretty."

"We hope he keeps his health," Doll says.

"He'll keep his health or he won't, goddamnit." Amanda stands up and turns around once. "Next week, bring him along. All right? We'll go walking." Amanda is smiling her flat-lipped smile. "So—" she says, leaning toward Doll. She chinks her teacup to Doll's glass. "—to your daddy!"

Doll swallows the water and she keeps her eyes on Amanda, who's sitting again and pressing the tips of her fingers against her eyebrows. Steam from the teacup rises, fans out, and blurs most of Amanda's face.

Doll squints her eyes to focus. When she sets her water glass down on the table, she sees a lipstick mark on the rim of the glass, and where she held it to drink, she can see the print of her fingers, even her palm.

How Many Boys?

Before they sat down to supper, the phone rang. The father picked up the phone on his way to his chair.

"Is the boy back from the paper?"

It was a woman's voice—nasal, insistent.

"What?" said the father. "One of our boys?"

"Is the boy back from the paper?" the woman asked again. It was the same tone and it made the man think of the phone company's recordings.

"You must have the wrong number," the father said, and hung up.

"Who was that?" asked his son.

"Some woman wanted to know if the boy was back from the paper."

"What boy?"

"Who knows? It didn't make sense. Maybe it was some kind of recording," the father said.

"Recordings don't call, do they?"

"Well, I don't know."

"What paper?" asked the son.

"Maybe she meant the newspaper," the father said.

"What boy went to the newspaper?"

"I don't know! She didn't say. I thought she meant you, or your brother, but you're both here. I don't know what she was talking about," the father said.

"I'm here," the boy said.

"Where's your brother? He's upstairs, isn't he?" The father called to his wife in the kitchen and asked if their other son was upstairs.

"I don't know," his wife said.

"Supper!" the father called. In a minute, when he heard no answer, he walked to the bottom of the stairsteps and called again. "Supper!"

"Did he go to the paper?" the boy asked his mother as she brought in a bowl of yams and set it on the table.

"What paper?" the mother asked.

"A lady that called asked if the boy was back from the paper."

"What paper?"

"We don't know," said the father, joining them. "Son, where's your brother?"

"I thought he was upstairs," the boy said.

"Supper!" the father called once more, loudly. He put his hands on his hips and turned slowly from side to side and looked up at the ceiling, listening.

"I heard something!" said the brother. "I'll get him."

He ran upstairs, two steps at a time.

"He's here!"

"Ah!" the man sighed to his wife. His lips parted and he almost smiled.

"It's a wrong number, for God's sake," she said. "We get them all the time."

"You get called about little boys, out on errands this time of night?"

"No, but it's always something. People just start in. She didn't realize you were a wrong number," she said.

"I don't sound like somebody else. She was upset," he said. "She called whoever she called because she was worried the boy was late."

"Good. Then she'll call the right number and find out."

"He was under his desk," said the boy, coming back into the room.

"I found a millipede," said his brother. "What should I do with it?"

"Out the back door," said the father. "Supper's about set."

The mother brought in a platter with a rolled boneless roast. She set a fat orange yam on each plate, and then she poured tall glasses of milk out of a plastic container.

"Get some napkins," she said to one of the boys.

He went to the cupboard and picked out four paper napkins. As the family sat down at the table, he tossed a napkin, sidearm like a Frisbee, toward each person's plate.

"Stupid," said his brother.

"Boys," said the father. "Just eat."

It was a pleasant meal. The mother and father talked about how many major appliances had failed in the year since they moved into the new house. The father said he knew the statistics for such occurrences.

"This *should* be our last," he said.

The boys shaped large lakes in the center of their mashed yams. They smoothed the rims with their spoons. Then they filled the lakes with the brown gravy, and drank the gravy spoonful by spoonful, out of the middle.

"Well, let's make up our minds about this dishwasher," the man said to his wife.

"Well, *get* it," she said. "I'm using two towels now for the leak. This one's not worth fixing." She wiped her lips and the end of her nose with the paper napkin.

"Maybe the lady said, 'Is the boy back *with* the paper?' " one of the boys said.

"She said it twice. She said *from* the paper," the father said.

"I bet he's a paper boy out on his route," the son said. "The newspaper office wouldn't be open."

"Well, let's hope she found him," said the father.

He crumpled his napkin in his palms, shaped it into a ball, and set it on the table. And since it was no longer dusk, but dark enough for him to see his reflection clearly in the dining-room window, he walked to the living room and turned on two lamps.

The house glowed.

When the father sat down in an easy chair, one of his sons climbed in beside him. The father put his arm around the boy so that the two would fit together just right.

The father kissed the boy's hair.

"So *here* you are," the father whispered.

The mother and the other boy cleared off the table. They rinsed the dishes and loaded the dishwasher. When the table and the counters had been wiped off with a damp rag, the mother set two cloth towels on the floor in front of the dishwasher and pressed the button to make the machine go.

The boy in the kitchen waited in the kitchen doorway until his mother walked by. Then he flicked off the kitchen light. He had taken one step toward the living room when the phone on the wall behind him rang. He jumped to the side and called out, "Telephone!"

The father leaned forward sharply, halfway rising. The boy in the chair beside him slipped backwards and sank against the coarse fabric.

With uninterrupted step, the mother turned and walked back to the phone. "Wrong number," she predicted.

"Just get it," said the father.

"Hello?" said the mother.

"Ma!" It was a child at the other end of the line.

"Hello!" the mother said loudly.

She turned her back to the living room.

"Who are you calling?" she said.

"Ma!" the child cried.

"You have the wrong number," the mother said slowly, clearly. "Hang up and try again. This is not your mother."

"Ma!"

"You must hang up the phone now and dial again. All right?"

The child cried, "Ma!"

"You must hang up the phone. Just dial the telephone again. I'm hanging up now. Good-bye," the mother said.

"The boy! Was it the boy?" the boy in the kitchen asked.

"It sounded like a baby," the mother said. "Some baby dialed a number."

"It was crying?" asked the father.

"It sounded like crying. It just said the same thing," the mother said.

"Call the police!" said the boy in the kitchen.

"What?" said the mother. "What for? They don't trace calls that have already hung up. How could they find the baby? Maybe it just plays with the phone."

"You said it was crying," said the father.

"It said ma," the mother said.

"A child knows how to dial for help," said the father. "Maybe it was hurt. Couldn't it talk?"

"I don't know how to dial for help," said the boy in the chair. He sat up and looked around.

"The kid was trying to call its mother and it got the wrong number. That's all," said the mother. "He'll dial again and get her."

"Maybe he's lost at the paper!" said the boy in the kitchen. He looked off toward the window, out toward the night.

"This was a baby," said the mother.

"It dialed a phone," said the boy. "Maybe he's *at* the paper, and it's closed up."

"Babies don't go on errands to the paper," said the father. "People shouldn't leave a baby alone like that."

"It's probably in its parents' room, thinking it'll call them up on the other phone," said the mother.

"They'd hear it!" one son said.

"Of course," said the father, nodding to his boy. "I think if the baby was crying, it was trying to call its mother."

"That's certainly all that he said," said the mother.

"Was the baby a boy baby?" one son asked.

"I don't know," said the mother. "It sounded like a boy."

"Maybe it couldn't turn on the lights," the other son said.

The family was quiet for a time. One boy went to look out the window. The mother went into the living room. She straightened cushions and sat down in the middle of the red sofa. A hearty smell of beef and gravy lay over the air in the rooms.

The boy at the window rubbed his breath from the pane. He rubbed again. Then he went to the kitchen and switched on the light.

"Well, should I call the police?" he asked. He reached for the phone on the wall.

"No," said his father. "There's nothing they could do."

"Can't we call somebody? There's two boys lost. Isn't that what there is?"

"How many boys?" one boy said.

"Those were wrong numbers!" said his mother firmly. "We get them all the time. They'll dial again and get who they want."

"It's almost time for the news," said the father.

They took their places. They sat together. The family sat together, and listened.

The Mechanics of
Good Times

Nice car." I start with that, through our open windows.

"It ain't mine," she says, mad.

But her lip swings up past a lost-now-forever front tooth and, for me, it's half of a lucky smile.

I don't mind flaws.

It's a breeze she stirs, from the cool of her mouth. Look at her now. What a tongue could do in that sad space—could push, could coax between good enamels.

She pulls in her head, winds up the car window, and gives me another smile.

Behind the glass, she is on display.

She has black eyebrows and thin black hair, too short. Her teeth that are good seem sturdy, fairly wide, with grooved edges. She is not one to grind her teeth when she drives through town,

I see that, or when she dreams her Prattville dreams, her head in the pillow and early gray light on her eyelids.

Well, the world, too, has lost its tooth. And its root—in night-time collision.

She's wise not to fill in the gap.

It shows her acceptance.

And she smiles again, at the generous thought; I believe she reads it, so kindly it is. In my truck, I turn my head and smile to the west, angling one narrow space, between my top left incisor and next bicuspid, in her direction.

Her head nods. I think it's a nod.

I don't turn my large front teeth to her.

No effrontery.

Or she'd duck with her chin, wouldn't she? And muscle her lips directly shut—oh, the wormlike cramp of lips as they tighten—and who would the girl be then in her green Camaro?

She works the ignition and doesn't look back. I follow her out of the parking lot, and, sure, she turns left without the turn signal.

She's going for beer.

On Railroad Street, shells of cars fire by—pickups and green vans; the usual blue hatchbacks. The world is in color again, in action, with Queen Anne's lace rampaging in ditches. How a gap-toothed girl can alter the motion of Friday dusk! It is this kind of thing that keeps you away from the local news—flings your hand right back from the TV knob with a pull at the elbow that sends your arm out like a wing.

The girl is easy to follow. Hand over hand on the wheel, she turns to the Three Corners Party Store and Union 76—OPEN, SELF-SERVE—and she chooses the center silver pump where there's also a hose for me. She prepares, I think, to notice the door of the white truck opening.

I step out gently from the dark of the cab. Easy. The heavier the tread of the shoes, the more graceful I am, I'm aware. And she notices. Look, she does not close her lips, and I approve of such thoughtlessness at such times.

Well, in plain view, she is wider than one would like, wide at the waist, wider again at the thighs, slung breasts pointing down to her knees. This is true. But, oh, the lost pink and rose of her small face! The lost white and baby-bright tooth, spat—I am guessing now—from the soft pink hold of the heart. It causes a swallow.

"Like a ride?" I say. "It's smooth."

"I'm getting gas. Period," says she, and she holds both hands on the latch of the nozzle.

Her Camaro lies low, muddied, and fills up with gas. She drives the dirt roads—that's fine with me.

She looks up. With cornering eyes, her hazel eyes, the girl takes in the truck.

It's a truck. I keep it up good. Why not? The world won't. And I comb my hair, too, why not? Sometimes you can find a girl who appreciates minor devotions, attention to the simple mechanics of good times.

"We could drive to Medina, and be back in an hour," I say to her, and it's possibly true. "Go ahead. Leave your car here."

She tops off the tank, squirt, squirt, and then she softens her arms and lets both white-sweatered shoulders drop. She'll be saying okay.

"Okay," she says. "Why not?"

Why not. Why not. She is my very girl. That's the brand of turned-over living, the circumspect zest that I know by heart. We permit life to go as it goes. Let the TV flicker. Let squirrels hoard nuts. We're taking the truck to Medina.

Some roads through farmlands, especially in August, are about as good as a road to heaven, and Medina Road is one of them, a surveyor's line, a farmhouse every half-mile on either side. Between houses run long fields, the corn parallel to the road. Very simple. Medina itself isn't much of a destination, but it happens to be the point where Bean Creek makes a U-turn, in the damp Medina Township Park. It's worth seeing, and the creek runs fast there, and the pines give out a strong scent by the water.

The place is not scenic—it's a half-moon of trees in the fields—but I have several good memories. My grandmother took me there sometimes when I was small. I remember how after she'd married her second husband, they'd slip in the water, I'm not sure wearing what, and they'd toss me back and forth, one to the other, until one of them, for a surprise, let me sink between hooped arms. I'd land on the brown silt of the bottom, then rebound like a baby, a bubble, to the stirred surface. Never in danger, I was a toy in the game of a festive couple. Why not, they probably thought.

Then they'd spray me with insect spray, head to foot, and we'd walk along the stream bank, meandering. My grandfather would lift me high on his shoulders for a ride, while he pulled my grandmother so close to him that my bare foot rested on her small breast whenever they'd lean against each other, whispering.

"I'm Alice," she says to me.

I never would have guessed it.

"Robert," I say, returning myself like a gentleman to my full name.

We're driving a length of road where, with speed, the corn stalks outside of Alice's window rush into one blur—yellow and brown near the roots; a grayish space above with the shadow of leaves; then darker green up the stalk; and upward to glittery yellow again, where the tassels stream in loosest bloom. The window above that is a smear of blue. All this I see behind Alice. She keeps her eyes like a serious girl on the gray road ahead.

"You work in town, Alice?"

"Yeah, I cook. What do you do?" Her lip slides up, and I sink once again into the lap of that half-curled smile. It lets me right into her mouth, her face, openhearted. With a tooth in place, you'd get nowhere. You wouldn't want to.

"Well, what do you do, Robert? Talk to me."

She's at ease enough to pretend to nag.

"I talk to myself," I say. A tyrant. But, crushing that tone, I go on. "I have been talking to myself, Alice. About you. Since I saw you in the parking lot."

She is attentive now. She shifts herself in the seat, with her elbow out the window, and her back presses against the door. She widens. Her left knee, bent like a bald head out of white pedal-pushers, crooks on the seat, and her body smudges—white below, a loose white sweater and obvious white bra, perceptible folds of flesh at the waist.

She says, "So what were you saying to yourself?" in a falling voice, letting me know she expects the usual story, the usual lies, she doesn't care, and she won't be impressed, no matter what.

I am honest, and therefore I almost tell her the truth. About that space between her teeth. But I'm not sure of everything yet. Which leads me to tell her the next-best thing, an underplayed sort of lie, set in as close as I can place it.

"I was telling myself," I tell her, "that I'd like to stir my hands in your hair."

"That's sweet," she says.

This she means. She touches her very thin, dark, very short hair.

"You married?" she asks, a necessary matter.

"I was. Twice."

"I was once," she says, and adds, as she should, "Your hair is nice, too."

Collaborators, we smile at each other our honest smiles.

The side gravel road into Medina Park drops downhill into a parking area at the edge of open ball fields, where leggy and speeding men run the infield, half in red T-shirts, half in blue. This Friday evening, family and fans gather on lawn chairs along the first- and third-base lines, or they sit with red Thermoses and beers on the picnic tables moved up behind home plate. Evergreen trees, dark hemlocks, rise some distance off on three sides and, far under the trees, children chase each other among twisting, rubber-seated swings. Everything moves.

Nobody takes note of our arrival, although it feels to me like a true event, which people should turn to, the way they turn to an opened door when they feel the breeze.

I take Alice's hand.

The park is damp after two days of rain, with shallow and gravelly puddles in every depression of the parking area. Alice and I step lightly. Over at the game, people sit on towels or on yellow windbreakers. Pushing our arms like swimmers, we head off toward the creek through waves of mosquitoes visible in the air. There is already deep shade near the water, which flows by, chocolaty from silt, holding barely within its banks.

"*Here's* all the rain!" Alice says.

She goes ahead of me, an explorer, walking with wide steps, although her legs are not long. She walks stretching herself toward the creek, and when she reaches the bank, she paces one way, then back, then farther one way, then back—ranging.

I lean like a supervisor into the trunk of a tree.

She bends to pick up an ice-cream stick, and a pink plastic cup, and these she pitches into a trash barrel that she passes. She still has the glance of a child, and the randomness of a child's attention. She throws out a flat stone.

In town, somebody else takes care of her kids, no doubt, and they play this same way. By the end of the evening, I suppose I'll know who they are, and where. But I have never minded the predictable character of life. When I drove back into this part of the state, it's true, I didn't remember much. But I've learned to recall, to predict, now that I'm back. Why not accept the circumstances, the plights?

For one thing, the women here don't expect much; they are realistic. They know that the Prattville men grow up disadvantaged—they have only the dogs and two blocks of sidewalks. They don't develop. And even if men from the farms are brighter, and better-looking, they are mute, which is probably sadder. A lover must say, after all, one or two things.

I find it easy to talk to women. I have a white truck, for God's sake, and I rent half a house.

I'd be concerned about Alice, sticking around. She has her strength, I can see that. But if she stays here, one thing's certain: She'll weaken. She will grow fat. It wouldn't be right.

Down by the stream, Alice is talking. She says her friend Roxie is good with crafts and has shown her how to glue pine needles and flower petals and lichen together, to make a fake scene out of nature.

"I have no time for destructive crafts," I say.

"Destructive? Making one thing out of another you call destructive?"

She likes the craft shows, she says. There's one in Coldwater tomorrow.

So, Alice would not make my days or nights smooth. She would fritter with this and that, keeping busy. But at the same time, I believe I could stare and stare into her face.

At the edge of the water, Alice pulls my arm. "Come on in." She's rough, as if I were local.

I say, "Alice, I've been to Detroit."

"And that makes you some kind of brain child, afraid of the water?"

But, truly, I think it's a good thing that she's not impressed. I think she admires the truck, but probably because it is white and she knows a white truck proves something in Prattville, and on the farm. She acts very tough, but she makes it her business to show gentleness, too. I see that. She turns her head slowly away, as if she is hiding, or is already hidden.

I say, "Alice, what's this? A crick. Have you seen any one of the Great Lakes?" But she turns away. She looks at her feet the way a beauty queen looks at her feet, seeing them. Then Alice takes off her sandals.

Prattville, I have discovered, is a place you can find such a woman, one who is first of all glad for a trailer. Which is not, I know, a pretty quality. But it is a good indication of this virtue— namely, the lack of wishes. I look for that finally. But I know that wishlessness is not stupidity. To be wishless is to be *ready*— for me, for instance; for come-what-may. Alice, I'm sure, does not dream of kitchens or pastel knitting.

She arranges her empty sandals, one by the other, and she drops her legs into the water. A brown spray kicks up around her knees and splatters dark drops on her white clothes. It's hard to believe how simple it is. Just look at her.

Everything that happens, ordinarily, leads a person to think

that there's no use trying; that something like picking up Alice—
who has her trailer, I bet, who has her two kids, who is easygoing—that picking her up is nothing.

But that's what I've learned to ignore.

Some things make sense, and I believe my life in the long run
will work itself out. I am honest, for one thing, and almost as
wishless as Alice. The way she drifts into things is appealing. So
I wonder, does she drift out?

I have the truck, and it could be easy.

Well, there goes Alice, into the water.

She strides. She's wet to her hips, and headed out into the
stream.

"Hey! There's a drop there! Alice, watch it!"

"I know!" she yells, and doesn't look around.

She's on her own. She walks forward, and there she goes, in
up to her waist, very slowly. You'd never know she had anything
else in mind than a stroll with a WALK sign, this side to that. It's
muddy, but that's not what she's thinking, and the water rushes
around her in braided rolls.

Looking at her, I have to admit, other things disappear. It is
quieter, darker. She won't go under, I know that. I'm afraid I will
have to wait a long time for her to come back. She is cooling,
cleansing, I suppose I could say. She'd dunk if she got religion,
and wear a white dress. Her steadiness looks just about like beauty:
Alice walks in up to her neck.

Then she turns around. Her small face is smaller than ever.
Without a body, the woman's extremely frail.

Under the water, a whiteness gives, and she is a lost thing
afloat.

I tell you my knees are shaking.

She smiles at me. It's the face of a girl of seven, her tooth
beneath her pillow.

It should be clear. With someone like Alice, I have to sit down, she takes my heart. Listen to this, I'm having a hard time breathing.

I don't really know what I'd do for the girl. But right now I think she could name it.

At First It Looks
like Nothing

It's dark here now, and how long it will be before anybody says *Jesus sweet Jesus* to me I don't know. Another shut-down day and what a beauty. I picked up two dried-out mice by the tails, opened the back door, and sailed them out flat into the snow. They were in the cellar, where I go when the pipes freeze to plug in the heat tape. It was zero all day, the sun round, the light like knives. Winter is mean metal in Michigan.

I'm in Michigan, but not, thank God, in a trailer.

There *are* houses in Michigan, like mine—houses with aluminum siding and metal-frame thermopanes. There are orchards around here, but other wood is gone, and all the small factories are stamping out sheet metal, and aluminum that shines a dullish shine and holds thumbprints. When a freeze touches houses, it's winter for good. The metal contributes to cold, and in a couple

115

of months Michigan houses help pull down the air in those low
bitter ground systems that hit Lake Erie and finally push off across
New York. The state's a significant factor in weather.

Durango, who is not, I'll say this, a cowboy, stops by after
supper. I'll tell him about the mice, and about the neighbor
whose dune buggy broke through the ice of the swamp at noon
and which is still in there, keeled forward.

We'll walk. We'll talk all evening.

Durango is bald, and won't wear caps, which means we walk
until he's using both hands and fingers, pressed to his head. It's
then we turn back.

We like the same things, Durango and I, and I like his wife,
Sybil.

Durango's from somewhere else and doesn't resemble Michigan men, who run their lives on motors, like twenty-first-century
jet-shooting backpackers, bodies in mechanized flight. Michigan
men have to move. They gather their gear and go. They can't
reminisce. Not many human beings in the world understand
them.

Durango and I try. If you're here awhile, you have to try—or
your husbands will rip the embroidered FAMILY off of their denim
jackets and go on a tour to Arizona with the kids.

Durango's wife, Sybil, his second, spent most of her teen-age
years on the back of a bike, and the world, she says now, stopped
at every red light.

On a walk, not much moves.

Sybil won't come along. She stays inside with *Woman's Day*.
She's tried to learn to crochet. She leafs through a magazine
back to front, then front to back, with a drifted look on her face,
like a kid in a grass field watching the wind. She's not old enough
to know she has memories, and nothing's happening now. In
another year she'll be back with the Walkup brothers and all of
that crew, gone to the dunes for long, nearly sexless nights.

They'll roll, the whole crowd, down the dunes together and then go through joints.

Durango and I will talk it all over.

When I tell Sybil in a year she'll be gone, she goes pale and unbends her knees, shakes her whole head of fine black hair, and says, "Maybe." When I tell Durango in a year she'll be gone, he pushes sand with the toe of his boot, and says, "It's the god-damn truth. I can't keep her."

I haven't kept anybody either. But in Michigan, that doesn't matter.

Durango and I are good for each other, no question about it. We walk; we make the slowest and longest love in the state. It's a love like the care of the dead, like the last wash—full of pity.

Tonight he's bringing some old-fashioned 3-D cards he found at a garage sale. I have my grandmother's wooden viewer, with the curved blind box like a small room around the eyes, where you go in, see the black-and-white pineapple fields in Hawaii and the field hands with machetes. I have stacks of the travel-geography series—mostly tropical, mostly huts and things grow-ing.

On the phone Durango said his cards are hand-tinted religious scenes. There's one of the tomb of Christ, he said, the rock rolled away and nobody in sight. Another, he said, shows the Rock of Ages in a stormy sea, with a ship on the side going under, and people in long robes drowning, and an arm, he says, reaching up from the water, the fingers almost touching the rock.

The last time we looked in the viewer, it was the summer and he had just met Sybil. We went out on the back steps with beer and a stack of cards, my grandmother's.

"You know Sybil."

He wanted agreement.

"You know how she looks, as if she can see things. The blanks people carve out of air."

It was true.

He said, "She could be anything."

That's what he liked.

"You'll be nothing to her," I told him. "She won't like you watching."

"I just want to kiss her thighs," Durango said.

"All right, then," I said.

We talked some more about Sybil, and looked at the laden banana trees, the stilt houses in the Congo estuary.

"Where's Marlene?" I asked him.

"She's with the Full Circle. I miss the noise," he said. Then he said, "Hunter?"

"I don't know. No word."

Then Durango smiles, with the large front teeth angled in. It's a passable smile.

Neither of us has much feeling for the other. We just seem to like the same things, and understand why so much fails.

That time I saved the best card for last, a miracle view of a quail's nest under weeds. In three dimensions, you look through the high grass to a rounded space underneath, where the camouflaged female sits with four chicks.

At first it looks like nothing.

Then we went for a walk and smelled the smell of the late alfalfa, the scent rising from our knees—faintly, the way memories come up, and keep coming, and pass through thought. When we took off our shirts and lay down there, it was like going under, the dropping away that feels in your legs like return.

Durango and I get drunk sometimes, talking too late. We keep track of each other and help out, whatever happens. When they stitched my neck, he brought me turtleneck sweaters and read me three books through three days. I've taken care of him too, when Marlene locked him out and turned up the amps, turned on every large and small appliance in the goddamn house.

We go out, after hard rain, to see how things stand, or to watch this show: the flaking down of cattails into the swamp, the collapse through light of real glitter. We're not the only ones walking around. There are animal tracks all over this farm.

Years from now, Sybil will probably be back with Durango. He's right—she can look through things, without thought. She sees all the white space in the magazines. The Walkup brothers will give her more time, more clear, unexceptional skies. I think Durango should try not to lose her; she has a fine, a tender laugh, her own melodious complaint.

Not many people in Michigan make it to eighteen without knowing how to drive.

"I've learned how to *ride!*" Sybil says. Her laugh swings around.

"Durango, take her on trips. Take some weekends." I said this last week, before the snows hit and before I knew it was winter.

"She'd say no. She'd say there's nothing she wants to see."

He was right. That's just what she'd told me.

I can see the dune buggy stuck in the swamp, a disaster of pipes and shadows in moonlight. At noon I heard the ice crack and saw the thing sink out there, the sun knocking long flashes off the roll bars. Durango will be interested, especially now that it's frozen in, the big tires nearly buried.

We'll probably walk out there, climb into the cold seats, and drive, drive—Durango hooahhing and me smacking some wild whip. The metal won't budge, and we'll lean like maniacs.

Someday Sybil would ride this out too, although now she'll say, shaking her hair, her eyes looking past the wheels, "When is thaw?" She is serious about men, the engines that drive them, as if they got her somehow to towns, to life, extremes of weather.

"She talks like Michigan," Durango says. "But you see those Kentucky eyes."

That's luck. Kentucky has streams, good drainage. When everything flows downhill, you learn to stand and watch and appreciate.

You don't drive like an idiot into the water.

Durango and I speculate about Michigan. Gossip. The way you would talk about husbands and wives, what they've done to your heart. We talk about Sybil, a daughter. Hunter, a son. And the rest. There's no end to the ruin.

Any number of nights, we walk the ground. We talk like two archeologists about the species. Then we sit in the dark like diggers in the light—khaki-shirted and squatting.

The Alvordton Spa and
Sweat Shop

Marabelle is embittered. She is a stylist, Marabelle of Marabelle's Beauty Bar. She's done all right. But her dreams of a carpeted house will always weigh her down. "This is not luck," she says.

"You have two good rugs," I say.

"Lucky to have two rugs?" She digs her toes in the purple nylon plush until I can hear her toenails scrape the jute backing.

"How's the baby?" I ask.

"Baby Lynn"—Marabelle answers loudly, sucking in her cheeks—"is not content. It's baby's name. I say, 'Baby, it was your father's idea. And so was Alvordton, Ohio.'"

"You tell the baby that?"

"I tell the baby everything."

Marabelle leans back in her nubby sofa. We're in the windowless basement, which is her whole house. The main floor and second floor, the designer kitchen and video-game room, never got built. And won't. Outside, when I came in, the second blizzard in two weeks was working itself up into something substantial, and inside, the rims of snow around the soles of my insulated boots melt into Marabelle's rug.

"Listen," I say. "I need help, Marabelle. I came for help."

"You?" she says, and she hands me a cup of cocoa. "Lynn, you want cocoa?" she yells toward a far door.

There's no answer. But we hear the rolls of wind across the huge concrete floor that is Marabelle's roof. When a gust catches around one of the ventilating grids curtained with burlap, lines of snow puff inside and fall behind Marabelle's sofa. The room is dark, although this is the middle of day. In her basement, Marabelle has one floor lamp, by my chair; it's a heavy, old-fashioned brass lamp with a deep, fringed shade.

"Marabelle," I say. "Look at me, Marabelle."

Marabelle, bony and pale, her eyes ringed with shadow, stares; she points her manicured, purple nails at me. "You cut your hair! Sweetheart, what *is* it?" Her mouth opens, "Ah," pityingly. She presses her fingers lightly against the tips of her own hair, which is fluffed and brushed toward the back of her head.

Marabelle is vain, as hairdressers have to be.

"Red cut his hair, too, don't forget," she says, "the day before he left. He pulled it all back in his left hand and he cut twice. My God. Be very, very careful what you do these next few days. Look at that." Marabelle points to the upright piano against the back wall; a saw handle sticks out toward us, halfway through the piano. "He couldn't do it," she said, "but he got far enough. He's in Houston, for God's sake, and he looks out his window into the trunk of a palm tree. He's gone too far. They have palm trees in Houston. He says that on New Year's Day he sat in a folding chair on green grass in his back yard!"

Marabelle is breathless. She lifts her bare feet off the rug and pushes them into the abyss between the sofa cushions. With her Gold Glow hair falling forward around her face, Marabelle hugs her knees and breathes in short puffs. "He claims he's with someone solid now."

"Marabelle," I say. "I need a place to stay."

This has happened before. When there's trouble, and I want to break down the issues and somehow stay intact, I get myself into a corner of Marabelle's basement for as long as it takes. JoAnn and Samina have done time here, too. The treatment works. JoAnn eventually decided to drive home to Pittsburgh. She's still with her parents, and maybe she always will be. Samina, after two days, decided to finish her Ph.D. and then go into the U-Pick strawberry business with Raymond, her lover of sorts. It all worked out. Marabelle, however, doesn't think of solutions and change that way. She watches us heal, but it makes her mad. And her attitude is taking its toll: she is shriveling, faster than the rest of us, with long dark lines that sometimes look painted from the corners of her eyes to the corners of her mouth. Her shoulders slump. She sucks anguish, like lemonade through a straw, all for herself. But, then, she has nowhere to go; she lives here. It's understandable—when you walk up the steps out of Marabelle's place, you feel taller; your skin feels slapped and toned.

"The Alvordton Spa and Sweat Shop," Samina wrote as thanks in a note to Marabelle, "gets four stars."

"She'll be back," Marabelle said, very sour.

I'm not sure what would please Marabelle. Not success in her work, or money. She already has the respect of Alvordton, for creative hairstyling. The Drift, her specialty last year, gained real notoriety, and Marabelle even drew in a few one-time customers from Toledo and Angola. She's a professional; she explains what she does. "New Wave, see?" she says of her new cut. A stylist need not be stylish, she says, so long as she knows what she's doing.

The carpeted house Marabelle dreams about—she says she dreams of it nightly—sounds like a house of horrors, all peach and magenta. The carpet goes up the walls. Marabelle laughs, clamping her lower lip with her front teeth. "I want it because I deserve it. Sure, I would hate it!" she says, and she lets the lines of her eyebrows soar.

She could have a decent house. She could have mine. But she stays where she is, in the cellar, through a bright February blizzard. It's a good basement, I admit, with a poured foundation. Red had connections.

"You're a fool," Marabelle tells me. "It's Mango, isn't it? He come at you with a knife?"

Mango is Mango Anderson, a man as mild, with a voice as mild, as anybody else from Michigan. But he does have black hair, which he parts in the middle, and wing-tip shoes, which he polishes. Marabelle doesn't really know him. She jumps to conclusions.

"Nobody came at me with a knife," I say.

Marabelle snaps her fingernails, the thumbs to each nail—left hand, right hand.

"Mango's in Traverse City. He's back in the orchards with his uncle. By spring, he'll be very happy. That's not the trouble. I'm here about something else. This is a problem with the world, Marabelle."

"Good," she says, and pulls on a pair of socks. "The world we don't have to cry over."

Marabelle gets out the extra blankets and I settle in. She has her routine: she takes Lynn to the sitter in the morning, works downtown at the Beauty Bar until five, and after closing she comes home with Lynn for soup and toast and ice cream. All day, I have the sofa, the blankets, the radio, a circle of yellow light from the fringed lamp, cream of wheat, milk, the works. I can let the drifts build around my car.

The first day, I sit on Marabelle's chair, wrapped in an afghan, and I listen to the wind. I cross my arms, push my fingers into my armpits, rest my palms on my breasts, and I listen. The wind is unsteady, gusting in large roars, machine noises, some of the time; or it hesitates, stumbles, before short, loud whistles. Through it all, I can hear the scrape of snow, like sandpaper over wood, slurring across the concrete roof.

I skip lunch. I skip the weather reports. I do some sleeping.

When Marabelle comes home with Lynn, they shake off snow and step out of their boots. Marabelle heats tomato soup.

"Well, what do you think?" Marabelle says.

"I don't want to be a parasite," I say.

Marabelle opens her mouth, an effect exaggerated for Lynn's sake, who runs around a chair. "You do no damage," she says. "Northern Ohio owes you thanks." She hands me a bowl of vanilla ice cream. "What do you know about parasites?"

"Too much," I say.

Marabelle knows I know too much: trematodes, fluke life cycles, the local Cheviot herds, and sheep mortality. I'm acting County Agent at the LaPier County Extension Office, since Harlin Baltodano lost himself in Peru six weeks ago. As far as we know, he's gone for good. I took over, and I like the job, even though work with farmers is not reassuring. There's trouble, disease, natural and unnatural crises.

"The human animal," I say, "destroys the body of nature. It's an interference, a worm."

Marabelle shrugs. "*Red* in Houston," she says, taking my dish, "is an interference. He chews on the female heart. Mango with his glittery eyes is an interference. Your farmers, my darling, pressure-hosing all their machinery—*they* are the interference. But a woman! A woman belongs to the planet!"

Marabelle has never had a subtle mind.

"You've had some hard times, Marabelle," I acknowledge.

"You said it," she says, and she winks at Lynn.

Marabelle invited Red to move in; she let him hang his John Deere cap on the hook; she let him use her phone to make his deals. He cheated on gravel tonnage and it was publicly known. Marabelle claims she didn't expect him to stay forever, or be civil, but she did expect him to build the upper stories of the house. Marabelle is certain everything evens out, sooner or later. It's an attitude that looks like weakness sometimes, but more often I see it as one kind of optimism: she thinks the world favors human life.

"Fight," Marabelle advises, shaking a fist. "Stop smiling," she tells me.

That attitude is part of the climate in Marabelle's basement. It's a wilderness, rancorous and spare, a good place to chuck out the usual sentiment and draw some conclusions.

Give me a couple of days, I told my office; I said I'd work on tracing Baltodano. Weeks ago, I did call the State Department and the consulate in Chicago. I did what I could, as a matter of fact. He may have decided to stay. Someone said he had family in Lima; and his last letter, in my judgment, was not that of a man ready to head home:

> I have gone out several days with local herdsmen. The lay of the land completely rules life (the land is Ohio turned on its side). But I am impressed with the grazing of marginal lands. One phrase here calls the practice "invisible farming." It is accurate. Karakul sheep the color of boulders graze steep slopes. And shepherds command real power. Stories in town connect them to

magic and to sudden bad weather. They walk into town,
bringing herds out of nowhere.

And so on. It's not just Baltodano. Alvordton is gradually emp-
tying itself of swindlers, babies, and everyone else. They go back
to nature, somewhere. Baltodano is typical. I've seen it too often,
and I don't intend to press the search much further.

Going away is tempting, of course—easy as walking away in
a blizzard, or losing your mind. You go out, and you don't come
back.

Through the first evening, Marabelle sits in her chair by the lamp
and looks through an old set of art books: *Art and Life in the
Americas; Masterpieces Through the Ages.* From these, she gets
ideas for hairdos, she tells me—Audubon has been helpful, too—
and she studies the pictures on every page with the bowed head
and sharply focused eyes of a scholar.

After an hour, she sets her books aside and reaches into a
sewing basket on the floor. With a heavy needle and dark heavy
thread, Marabelle starts to sew her two purple rugs together—
quick, loopy stitches. She's thinking a mile a minute, and she
isn't thinking about me. "It's unjust," she says, in good spirits,
as if in the center of conversation, as if I had already agreed with
her, "that vengeful assault is not legal." The word *vengeful* vi-
brates through her front teeth, and I can tell that to her it sounds
like music. "Unless you're in prison," she says, "the only choice
you have is to be in or out. If you're in Poland, you're in or
you're out. Alvordton, in or out. So, you stay or you leave."

"People get lost," I say. "Baltodano's lost."

"That's stupid. There's no such thing," Marabelle says. "Dead
is not lost; alive is not lost."

"Well, people lose touch."

"Sweetheart, you push. You say go. I've heard it. You probably said, Baltodano, enjoy yourself. See the sights. You said, Mango, *go*, didn't you? See what that does? What have you got? What makes you think anybody anywhere should do what he wants? Will I let Lynn go? *Never.* Will Red run along on his own? Not on your life." Marabelle lays the sewn rug pieces down in a long strip in front of the sofa. "Look at that!" she says to Lynn. "Think what your daddy would say about *that!* He'd have a fit," she says to me, satisfied.

I lean my neck back against the sofa. The wind is calm.

"Marabelle," I say, "this next agricultural tour—Czechoslovakia. They asked me to go."

"You?" she says. "Well." She is rubbing the seam in the rugs, meshing the yarns.

"The pamphlets show muckland," I say. "It looks like LaPier County."

Marabelle sits up straight. "So *you* might be taking off. Well, all right, go on; join the crowd. Lynn, tell her to go. See, I learn," she says, very bitter.

"Go," pipes up Lynn.

Then, like my overseer, Marabelle hands me my coat and sets my boots at my feet. "Storm's over," she says. "Let's stroll."

We plod through the drifts on the step, and go up. Alvordton in drifted snow, at dusk, is not quite picturesque, even to eyes accustomed to Marabelle's cellar. The dogs that stretch on their chains by garages have already dirtied a full circle, and too many windows—through which one sees tiny families, bent at the dinner tables—are sheeted with plastic pulled across the glass and tacked to the frames. Some of the plastic has frayed; but worse than the fraying is the plastic that holds, taut—it weakens the look of the windows; it coats the faces inside with a viscous film.

Stomping in rubber boots, Lynn walks between Marabelle and

me. We go down Church Street to the Beauty Bar, with its Style-Rite men and women posters in the window, their dark hairdos faded to blue.

"I'm getting some scissors," Marabelle says. She unlocks the front door.

Marabelle feels her way inside in the dark, and then switches on three rows of overhead fluorescent lights. There are half a dozen vinyl armchairs against one wall, and in an alcove in the back are the barber chairs, the mirrors, open drawers of combs and blue curlers. While Marabelle searches for the scissors, Lynn and I stand in the front looking at the walls, the way customers waiting their turn look at the walls. On some cork-board, Marabelle has tacked up photographs of the Hairdressers' Association Christmas Ball. There's a photo of Marabelle and Red outside the LaPier Holidome; more snapshots of them inside. At the entrance to the Holidome, between two pillars with greens twisted down and around them, Marabelle and Red lean together, under two red paper folding bells. Red wears high-heeled brown boots, a suede suit, and the white Stetson Marabelle gave him. In apparent honor of his name, Marabelle wears red; she stands very tall beside him, her dress long and full, draped with strings of red Christmas lights, like jewelry around her neck and sleeves. The lights are lit up in the photo. Another picture, taken inside, shows a close-up of Marabelle's hair, which is dyed Christmas-red, or maybe she dyed a wig and set the hair in long loose curls, with more lights woven in with the strands.

"When I pressed a switch in my hand," Marabelle explains to me, over my shoulder, "I lit up just like a star. Shocking," she says. "Red didn't mind."

"He's not a trustworthy man."

"He keeps in touch," she says.

She sticks a small gold scissors in her coat pocket. Putting up the hood on her coat, Marabelle turns off the lights in the shop, and we continue our walk, past Panda Service, with the pumps gone and SCRU-YOU spray-painted in orange on a cement-block wall; and then we're standing at the yellow blinker in the middle of town, where we cross to the Diamond Bar, to Sterling Hardware, and to Neal's Pro Shop, the one block of old brick buildings with double-story façades. The upper floors are dark.

Circling around through yards toward Marabelle's place, we pass houses set far back in drifts, like lighted huts. The air is cold, but I breathe it in, past my teeth. I imagine opening my mouth to speak and instead of hearing words that I'd understand, I hear the thick sounds of a Middle-European language tumble out, and Marabelle turns to me and answers in the same incomprehensible tongue.

No one speaks. Every now and then, Lynn presses full-force into our hands, jumps, and lands up ahead in the snow on both feet, with a sound like something breaking.

"I've got an idea for Valentine's Day," Marabelle says as we walk down the steps to her basement door. "Heart-cut bangs, a light set. The style would look terrific on you."

"I'll think about it," I say. She's trying to find a way to patch up the damage I've done cutting my own hair. "I'll give it some thought," I say.

And I do. There's plenty of time.

I sleep long nights. Days I'm awake, but as motionless as I can manage. Marabelle works—out in the morning, back at night. She talks with Lynn and leaves me alone. Under this care, it doesn't take long.

After five days, a reasonable time, when I'm feeling flesh on my bones again, I say to Marabelle, "Okay. Cut."

"I knew it."

She goes to a drawer and pulls out the gold scissors. I sit in the chair by the lamp, my arms flat, and I feel the press of fatty cells, reserves. In the distance, I hear the highway noises, trucks from the Pabst bottling plant, mail trucks. I hear my pulse, when it races, and when it lags. I decide: Tomorrow I get in my car and drive home.

"I'm on the mend, Marabelle," I say.

"I can see that," she says, and frowns. "Wonderful."

She stands behind me, in the shadowy light. All light is a luxury, she told me one time, explaining that the Beauty Bar only illuminated all the corners for the sake of the clients. The stylists, she said, could do their work in the dark.

Marabelle trims at my bangs. "Before you leave," she says, "you ought to know this—I've decided to go to Houston. Just a visit. It won't take long. You may be out on your tour, and I wanted you to know." She sets down the scissors. Her voice steams up. "See this?" Marabelle yanks a suitcase from under the sofa and opens it at my feet. She walks to a dresser along the opposite wall and from the top drawer she lifts up a hunting knife in a decorated leather sheath. Marabelle throws the knife into the empty suitcase and then she closes the latch and locks it.

"They have metal detectors now," I warn.

"I'm driving!"

"Mango said we should visit him up north in the spring," I tell her. "He says it's amazing, all the blossoms and the lake. You stand in the middle of the orchard and see the blue water, white flowers overhead. There's nothing to smell but sweet air. Marabelle, he says it'll make a person cry."

"He says." Marabelle kicks the suitcase. "You give men too much room," she says. "Every one—they go. Count them!"

She picks up the scissors again, and, gently, she lifts my hair in her fingers, and snips. When she's finished, she holds up a mirror for me. She's clipped the bangs in two little dips, a phony heart pressing upside down on my forehead. Marabelle's asking for trouble.

"An angel like me, on your shoulder," she says, "sees the heart." She struts around; she swoops her arms like wings.

So I laugh, and it doesn't strain any muscles. After all, Marabelle may be the next one out of Alvordton—she's tied to the scenery even less than most. Some people think they can come and go—Marabelle thinks she can come and go. She can swear all she wants that she'll come home. But I don't believe it.

The world the way it is, it's harder all the time to tell who's even planning to come back.

A NOTE ON THE TYPE

The text of this book was set in Electra, a type face
designed by William Addison Dwiggins (1880–1956) for the
Mergenthaler Linotype Company and first made available in 1935.
Electra cannot be classified as either "modern" or "old
style." It is not based on any historical model,
and hence does not echo any particular period or style
of type design. It avoids the extreme contrast between
thick and thin elements that marks most modern faces, and
it is without eccentricities that catch the eye and
interfere with reading. In general, Electra is a simple,
readable type face that attempts to give a feeling
of fluidity, power, and speed.

Composed by Crane Typesetting Service, Inc.,
Barnstable, Massachusetts
Printed and bound by The Haddon Craftsmen,
Scranton, Pennsylvania

Designed by Judith Henry